one word,

SIX LETTERS

ALSO BY ADIB KHORRAM

Darius the Great Is Not Okay

Darius the Great Deserves Better

Kiss & Tell

The Breakup Lists

one word, SIX LETTERS

ADIB KHORRAM

HENRY HOLT AND COMPANY
NEW YORK

Henry Holt and Company, *Publishers since 1866*
Henry Holt® is a registered trademark of Macmillan Publishing Group, LLC
120 Broadway, New York, NY 10271 • fiercereads.com

EU representative: Macmillan Publishers Ireland Ltd, 1st Floor, The Liffey Trust Centre,
117–126 Sheriff Street Upper, Dublin 1, D01 YC43

Library of Congress Control Number: 2025009282

First edition, 2026
Book design by Maria W. Jenson
Printed in the United States of America

ISBN 978-1-250-40555-5
10 9 8 7 6 5 4 3 2 1

For you, trying to find a way back.

PART 1

september

1
DAYTON

YOU KNOW YOU'VE MESSED UP WHEN YOU GET MARCHED INTO THE principal's office.

Not the little waiting area outside, where the bad kids—the troublemakers and class clowns and bullies—sit while they wait for the hammer of judgment to fall on them.

No. You're standing in the doorway of the principal's actual office.

You thought a high school principal would have a fancy office, maybe with windows and a mahogany desk or something, but this is just like every other part of the main office: gray walls full of pushpins, heavy wooden doors, black office chairs, and a tan desk that isn't made of real wood.

Dr. Matthews's office faces out to the rest of the main office, but the windows are coated with some sort of cling film that makes them all blurry, so you can't see out and no one can see in. One corner is peeling away from the glass.

Mr. Clemens, your ELA teacher, frog-marched you in here. You're not 100 percent certain what a frog march is, or where you heard the term, but you're pretty sure that's what happened. He deposits you in the chair across from Dr. Matthews's desk. It's metal, with a soft cushion for the seat, and it sinks beneath your weight. The fabric is so scratchy your butt itches through your shorts, but you don't scratch or shift, because even though Mr. Clemens isn't touching you, hasn't touched you at all, you feel like he's got a hand clamped on your shoulder, keeping you in place.

"It'll be a few minutes," he says. His voice is kind of high for such a burly guy, bald and round-faced with a full mustache. His brown skin turns pale in the fluorescent lights.

Your phone buzzes in your pocket. You wonder if you can risk a reach for it. It's probably your boys making fun of you for getting in trouble. Maybe telling you off a little, too. It wasn't cool, what you did, but you didn't mean anything by it.

You reach for your left pocket, but Mr. Clemens spots the movement.

"No phone."

You put your hand back in your lap.

Mr. Clemens hovers behind you, his gaze drilling a hole in the back of your head. Or maybe that's your imagination. Maybe he's on his own phone, doing a crossword puzzle or something, because teachers get to do that kind of thing. Students don't.

Your stomach grinds against itself, and you wonder if he can hear it.

The thing is, you never would've done it if Reggie hadn't dared you. You missed breakfast this morning. Marshall's been eating twice as much ever since football season started, so all that was left at home was your mom's gross organic-vegan-keto protein bars that she doesn't share anyway.

But Reggie bet you twenty dollars, and the Pop-Tarts in the

vending machine were calling your name. You've got a quiz in US history fourth hour, right before lunch, and you're pretty sure all your teachers from kindergarten through fifth grade talked about how important it was to eat a good breakfast before you took a test.

They stopped reminding you of that in middle school. And they stopped giving you recess, too. And now here you are, in high school, with no recess, and no breakfast, and no Pop-Tarts. Not even the twenty dollars Reggie promised you, because Mr. Clemens pulled you out of the assembly before Reggie could hand it over.

Your stomach gives another growl, and this time you're pretty sure Mr. Clemens notices because you can hear his feet shift.

There's a bowl of individually wrapped Life Savers mints on the corner of Dr. Matthews's desk in a little square bowl. You don't need a mint, even if they do make your mouth light up when you crunch them, but maybe it would stop your stomach from grumbling.

"Can I have one?" you ask. You're kind of surprised your voice still works, given how dry your mouth is. And your throat.

Mr. Clemens sighs, and you're pretty sure he's going to make you ask again and say *May I* instead.

"Take one and keep your mouth shut," he says instead. "You're in enough trouble as it is."

So you do, and the plastic crinkles so loudly as you pop it open. The embossed lettering on the top of the mint scratches the roof of your mouth, and the Wint-O-Green flavor makes your tongue tingle.

Then you're stuck again, waiting for Dr. Matthews to show up and pronounce your fate.

YOU'RE NOT SURE HOW LONG YOU WAIT. DR. MATTHEWS DOESN'T have a clock in his office, at least not one you can see from your chair. You don't have a watch (though maybe you should start wearing one, now that you're in high school). You reach for your phone to check the time, but Mr. Clemens reminds you, "I said no phone."

"Sorry." You swallow.

It must've been at least thirty minutes, though. The bell rang twice, once to dismiss second hour, again to start third. You're missing German, and you wonder if Frau will know where you are. If she heard about what you did.

Hot shame bubbles in your stomach. You didn't mean it, after all. It was just a joke. Reggie's idea. One word, six letters.

You didn't think it would be such a big deal.

But you should've known better. You realize that now.

Has Frau heard? You hope not. You really like her. She's probably your favorite teacher. Maybe it's because for some weird reason you're actually kind of good at German, even though you've never managed better than a B-minus in English. Or maybe it's because she calls you by your real name, Dayton, instead of making you (and everyone else in class) pick fake German names, so you don't have to go by Jörgen all year. Or maybe it's just that she seems happy to see you in class every day, when most teachers are somewhere between annoyed and indifferent.

You're not a bad kid, but you're not a teacher's pet, either. You do your homework, you try your best. Sometimes you do okay, sometimes not. It's not like your parents have time to help you. Marshall's always too busy with his friends, and even if he wasn't, he's always been smart, taking AP classes. It's not like he remembers what it was like to be a freshman trying to figure out high school when no one gives you a manual.

You really do miss recess.

And you could honestly use some time to run around a yard right now, because you keep wanting to jiggle your leg, but every time you do, Mr. Clemens clears his throat and you go still again. But it has to have been at least an hour, right?

Your stomach growls. You really could've used that twenty. And those Pop-Tarts. Even if they were out of the good ones and you had to get a mid flavor, like unfrosted strawberry. Worse, that mint made you even thirstier. Plus your mouth is fuzzy now.

Last year in social studies you did a whole unit on the Bill of Rights, and you're pretty sure this is against the Eighth Amendment. That was the *cruel and unusual punishment* one, you're pretty sure.

It was a while ago.

The door finally swings open, and you sit up straighter in the weird chair, which makes you itch again. Or maybe you're imagining it.

You can't stop yourself from looking over your shoulder, and—

Crap.

Crap.

No wonder it took so long.

Dr. Matthews called your dad.

Your dad's in his usual work uniform—a faded band T-shirt,

Nirvana in this case, and jeans that are a bit too big, but at least he put on actual shoes instead of going out in his Crocs again. Not that you have anything against Crocs, but camo? Really?

He works from home, though, so what can anyone expect? He didn't always—he used to work in an office, and you think you remember him wishing you a good day and hugging you goodbye as he left in the morning, back when you were really little—but it's been this way for a long time. Which is great, you guess. Except now, when he has to come into school. And it's not because you vomited in the middle of math class. It's because you messed up, big-time.

Your dad takes the seat next to you and runs a hand through his hair. It used to be blond like yours, but you only know that because of pictures. Now it's a golden brown, matching the neat, slightly pointed beard on his chin. His hair is messy, which means he didn't have any meetings this morning, or at least none worth styling it for. Including you.

He doesn't glance at you, though you try to meet his eyes. They're dark blue, the same color as yours. Everyone says you look like your dad. That you're a carbon copy of him back when he was younger, when they actually had carbon copies. Though maybe that was more your grandpa's time than your dad's.

Dr. Matthews tugs his shirtsleeves down where they're caught beneath his sweater. He sits behind his desk and nods to Mr. Clemens, who steps out and closes the door behind him. Then it's just you and your dad and the principal and that word you used hanging over all your heads.

Dr. Matthews looks from you to your dad and then back to you. He's younger than your last two principals, younger than your dad, even. You wonder if he got his PhD just last year. He's earnest-looking, though, not stern. His hazel eyes look big and sad, magnified in the thick lenses of his clear-framed glasses. His tanned white skin is freckled, and his thick, rust-colored eyebrows, which match his short-cropped hair, are always arched in a way that makes him look a little bit morose.

He sighs.

Why do adults sigh so much?

And why do they sigh so much at you, lately?

"So, as I told you earlier, there was an incident," he tells your dad.

Your dad finally looks your way, but this time it's you who avoids his eyes, staring at the painted-on wood grain of the desk in front of you. You wonder if you could get away with another mint. Your stomach growls again.

"You still haven't said what," your dad says, exasperated.

Dr. Matthews waits for you to fill in the silence, but you're too embarrassed to admit what you did.

Now that the challenge of Reggie's dare and the weird energy of the crowded assembly have faded, you don't even know why you did it anymore.

All you know is you shouldn't have shouted it. You didn't mean anything by it. You'd take it back if you could.

Another sigh.

"Our freshman English classes had an assembly today with an alumnus. Adam Markham. He's an award-winning poet who came back to give a talk on writing to our students."

"I see," your dad says, but it's clear he's never heard of this poet guy, either.

And honestly, you forgot he even went here. He graduated before you were born. He was basically a stranger. Looked like one, too, wearing a jacket and scarf even though it's still eighty degrees out, like he forgot what September is like in Kansas City because he lives out in California now with all the other fancy people who wear their pants way too tight and their shoes way too pointy and their shirts only tucked in on one side.

Sigh number three.

"Dayton here decided to disrupt Mr. Markham's presentation."

Now it's your dad who sighs. "I'm sure he's not the only kid who can't sit still through a long talk."

You're not a kid anymore. You're fourteen! You're in high school. But your dad refuses to treat you as anything but a child.

"Maybe, but he was the only student who shouted a slur at our guest."

That gets your dad's attention. You take a sly peek at him. His face is turning red and blotchy, which it always does when he's embarrassed.

You embarrassed him.

"What exactly did he—"

"I'm not going to repeat it, but everyone heard it. Thankfully, Mr. Markham was able to recover quickly, and we pulled Dayton out." He turns to you. "Dayton, do you have anything you want to say?"

You shake your head. *No.*

Except:

"Sorry."

And you are. Really sorry.

But it was just a word. You didn't think it would be as big a deal as it ended up being. You thought people would laugh it off and move on. You thought—

Honestly, you're not even sure anymore.

You've never said that word before. It's not like it's part of your vocabulary. But still, it was just a word.

Both adults wait for you, but what else is there to say?

You won't do it again. Obviously.

"That's it?" your dad asks. "You're sorry?"

A fourth sigh. Dr. Matthews is really laying it on thick, isn't he?

"As you may remember, you and your wife, and Dayton, too, signed forms acknowledging our district's zero-tolerance policy toward bullying. Under the circumstances—"

"Bullying?" your dad asks. "Dayton's not a bully."

You're almost surprised your dad defends you. But he's right: You're not a bully. You're not.

You made a mistake. If anything, Reggie was the bully. He tricked you into doing it. And he never even gave you your twenty dollars.

"His choice of language suggests otherwise," Dr. Matthews says, voice flat, and if it wasn't you in this scratchy chair, if it were some TV character and he was talking to a TV principal, you'd laugh at this part, because it came out kind of funny. Instead you cough to cover it up.

This whole thing is extremely unfunny.

"Okay, but he didn't say . . . whatever . . . at any of the students, right? So he might've been being stupid, but he wasn't bullying anyone."

You hate when your dad calls you stupid. Not everyone can be a network engineer with a photographic memory like him. He calls your brother stupid, too, sometimes. And he never says it mean, just as a statement of fact. Like he's discussing the weather. Like it's a given that no one around is as smart as him.

Still, Dr. Matthews presses his lips into a flat line and considers. Takes a breath, and, yup.

There's sigh number five.

"Regardless, there have to be consequences," he says. "Three days in-school suspension."

"Three days?" your dad nearly shouts.

"Or we can go with the seven days out-of-school that district policy mandates." For the first time, his voice sharpens, and you understand just how angry he really is. At you. For what you did.

"I'll do it," you say, surprised you can make your voice work. "The three days, I mean."

You finally meet Dr. Matthews's eyes. They don't look sad anymore; they look stern. He gives you a nod.

"All right. And if you ever do something like this again, I promise the consequences will be dire. Got it?"

You swallow.

"Got it."

2

FARSHID

YOU'RE SO USED TO PEOPLE SAYING YOUR NAME WRONG, YOU DON'T realize it at first. After all, people have been messing up *Farshid* for as long as people have been saying it. Even the teachers who get it (mostly) right can't quite do the *ar*, which is sort of halfway between *air* and *are*.

Add in the jumbled footsteps and slamming lockers and shouts of the C Hall during passing period, and you're honestly surprised anyone can hear anything at all.

So, yeah. You're used to it.

So used to it, it takes several seconds to realize what you actually heard.

You whip your head around to look over your shoulder but then face forward again, keeping your pace through the halls steady, because at this point you should know better than to let anyone know you heard them.

Don't react. That's the rule.

Don't let them know it bothers you.

And it doesn't, anyway, because what do they know? You're not gay, after all. At least you don't think you are, and even if you were, you wouldn't have told anyone, least of all anyone at school.

Why do you have to know yet, anyway? Six months ago, you

still had a LEGO fortress in the basement and your friends spent the night for *Mario Kart* tournaments and pancakes in the morning, but then this summer, it was like a switch flipped and your imagination flickered and died. All your LEGO adventures seemed childish, even *Mario Kart* seemed too easy, and everyone wanted to switch to *Fortnite*.

High school is even worse than you imagined. Half your classmates only want to talk about who's dating who. The other half, you don't even know, because they came from the other middle school that feeds Meadowbrook.

And meanwhile, last week Valerie Farrell started crying at lunch when her girlfriend dumped her while they were waiting in line for the salad bar. Brody Connors got in-school suspension for making a joke about *whacking it* in algebra yesterday.

Dayton Reilly got pulled out of this morning's assembly for shouting a slur at the top of his lungs. The same slur you just heard in the hallway. Were they talking about you? Were they just shouting it because they wanted to be edgy?

Or were they relaying the story of what Dayton had done?

After, as that word echoed in the auditorium, Dayton had waited, like he was expecting a laugh or something, but everyone had gone all quiet. Mr. Markham's presentation had been pretty good, a little funny even. You don't really care about poetry—even though Baba says it's in your blood—but Mr. Markham had some pretty good jokes, and he also talked about playing *Mario Kart*, so all in all it was a decent talk.

But still, this is nothing like middle school. No one seems like themselves anymore, except for you. You still feel like you're in eighth grade, other than the fact you grew taller over the summer, tall enough you had to get new clothes. You're too big to play with LEGO sets anymore, but you miss them anyway.

You think you hear it again. You're almost certain.

Whispers and laughs follow you as you slip inside the classroom, take your seat, and wait for the bell. Ms. Suchecki's stepped out of the room and hasn't come back yet.

Your hackles rise. You didn't know you had hackles, but that's what this feeling is, right? Maybe you're hearing it wrong. Maybe it's not you. Maybe they really are just talking about Dayton. You didn't realize he was a homophobe. You've known him since third grade, when you had to change schools because your family moved half a mile, which put you over the county line, which meant you had to say goodbye to all your old friends and make brand-new ones.

You've never been friends with Dayton, but he seemed fine. He never said anything meaner than anyone else. He let you borrow some lead when your pencil ran out last week. He should be here in US history right now, sitting behind you, but you saw him get pulled out of the assembly. Maybe he's still in the office. Maybe he got sent home.

You can't believe what he said.

One word. Six letters like daggers, shouted for all the school to hear.

So why does it feel like they're aimed at you?

"HOW'D YOU DO?" NOUR ASKS.

Her locker is right above yours, which is annoying, because she's like a foot shorter than you, so she has to go on her tippy-toes while you have to crouch, and it didn't occur to either of you to switch early on, and at this point hers is all decorated with magnets and stickers and you're both too used to things to change now.

Nour's wearing a keffiyeh over her vintage *Star Trek* T-shirt, her black hair pulled into a ponytail. You thought she might be Iranian, like you, when you heard her name, but it turns out Nour means "light" in Arabic, too, and she's Palestinian and Jordanian, not Iranian. Plus she was born here—her parents, too.

"We still caucus together, though," she had told you blithely as you talked about your backgrounds. "All from the 'terrorist-y' part of the world."

"Fair," you had answered, trying to pull off blithe yourself, but you weren't sure if you had or not.

You've gotten better since, so now you blithely answer, "At least a B-plus. You?"

"I think I messed up a couple, but I know I got the extra credit at the end right."

You nod. Thank God they still do extra credit in high school. You grab your orchestra folder out of your locker and stuff it into your backpack. You don't have orchestra until sixth hour, but it's on the other side of the building from the computer lab, where you have fifth hour computer science, so you don't have time to visit your locker. At least you don't have to lug your cello around—you keep yours at home and use one of the school's for class, even though it doesn't sound as good.

Nour stands on her toes to look in the mirror hung inside her locker door and apply some sort of tinted thing to her lips with the pad of her middle finger. You smell a hint of cherries before she screws the lid back on the stuff and drops it into her backpack. "Ready?"

You shrug your backpack to settle it and nod.

Nour's got bio next hour, but her class is close to yours, so you walk together through the press of bodies on all sides, freshmen weaving in and around tall seniors who have time to stand in place talking to one another because their lockers are actually close to their classes.

You hear it again—those six letters—but it's someone talking about Dayton this time. Nour must see those hackles of yours.

"That was awful, huh?" she asks. "The assembly."

"Yeah." You don't know what else to say.

Dayton never did show up to US history. Maybe he got sent home. Maybe he got suspended. Maybe he got expelled.

Whatever happens, he deserved it. Unless it was, like, a firing squad, but you don't think they do that in high school, not even in Missouri.

"I mean, I knew we had bigots here, but to just shout it like that, with all the teachers there . . ." She shakes her head. "What a butthead."

"Yeah," you say again, because there's something churning in your chest, and you can't quite decide what it is. But your heart feels a lot louder in your rib cage, as though its syncopated beats should be making your shirt ripple like the skin of a timpani when it's been struck. *Bumb. Bumb. Bumb.*

And then something hits you from behind, and you stumble, and for a second you wonder if getting beaten up is a thing that really happens to people in high school. You thought it was a myth. But then you realize it's another freshman, their backpack way too full and probably giving them scoliosis or something, barreling down the hall like an awkward Ninja Turtle trying to make it to the far end of the A Hall before the bell.

Nour catches you before you actually fall.

"Thanks."

She pats your back and looks after the retreating turtle. "Sure. See you?"

"Yeah. See you."

Nour keeps going, and you turn left at the cross hall for your computer lab, TECH 4, and though you've seen TECHs 1, 2, 5, and 6, you've never actually seen TECH 3. You're not entirely convinced it exists.

TECH 4 smells a little like burnt dust, like that first day when the heat comes on in the fall, and you wonder if maybe the computers need to be cleaned or something. The lab is in four rows, monitors and keyboards and mice (mouses?) on the blond desks, the towers themselves on the floor below at just the right height to bang that soft spot in your knee if you wheel your chair in at the wrong angle.

You take your seat at the far end of the second row, get signed in, log in to the portal to see if the grade from your history quiz is posted yet, but of course it's not, Ms. Suchecki probably hasn't even graded it yet.

There's one notification, though, from your student email.

The *From:* line reads *Dr. Henry Matthews, Principal, MHS.* Your heart does that *bumb bumb bumb* thing again, but you're not in trouble, right? It's not your fault if people are calling you names. Oh God, what if you cheated on your quiz? You're not sure how you could've, but maybe Ms. Suchecki thought you were looking at someone else's desk when you were really staring at the ceiling?

One month in and already flunking, and you didn't even do anything!

But no, the subject line reads *Today's Assembly*, and you definitely didn't do anything there, especially not compared to what Dayton Reilly did.

The computer lab is filling up. You're the only freshman in this class. You had to appeal to your counselor to skip Comp Sci I, because it was all stuff you'd known since seventh grade. One of the juniors in the back row is snickering, and your hackles, your brand-new hackles, rise again. Are they laughing at you?

When did you get to be so worried? So . . . afraid?

Maybe that's what the feeling in your heart is.

You're afraid.

Not just anxious. Or nervous. Or any of the other million weird things you've felt since you started high school and had to learn all new rules and a brand-new building and suddenly you were *grown-up* but not really grown-up because you still have to do what all the adults tell you, but now they think you're supposed to be *responsible* just because you're in ninth grade.

No.

Fear. Real fear. It's new and it doesn't feel good and you don't remember being afraid before, but now Dayton Reilly's shouting slurs for the whole school to hear, and people might be calling *you* a slur behind your back, and maybe they really do beat up gay kids here. And you're not even gay!

That doesn't matter to them, though. Whoever they are. The bigots and homophobes and all the people who don't like you because you're you, because you like computers and LEGO sets and your cello instead of boobs and *Fortnite* and *whacking it*.

The bell rings, but Ms. Walton is always a minute or two late because the hallways aren't exactly friendly to her wheelchair, so you swallow away your fear and read Dr. Matthews's email and hope that'll make you feel better.

It doesn't, though. You're not sure there's anything that could.

> To the students, parents, faculty, staff, and community of Meadowbrook High School,
>
> An incident occurred today during our assembly hosting Adam Markham, an award-winning poet and MHS alumnus who was kind enough to come speak to our first-year English language arts classes. That incident is inconsistent with our values here at MHS—values of tolerance, kindness, compassion, and integrity. I've already spoken to Mr. Markham to extend an apology on behalf of our entire school, but I'd like to take a moment to discuss in more detail what measures we're taking and how the Meadowbrook community plans to move forward from this . . .

3

Dayton

AS IF GETTING IN-SCHOOL SUSPENSION WASN'T BAD ENOUGH, you're also grounded.

Your mom and dad won't say for how long.

Your dad brought you home after the meeting with the principal. It didn't count as part of your suspension; Dr. Matthews just thought it was best you go home for the day, since it was already halfway through Friday by then and your dad had driven to school and all.

But now it's Saturday, and you're bored, stuck in your room without your Xbox or your phone. You don't even have any homework to do. You didn't get the chance to go by your locker before leaving. Your dad was eager to be gone.

He's already given you three different "How could you be so stupid?" talks. And your mom? Well, she gave you a long lecture about how *disappointed* she was. How she *didn't raise you to speak that way*. But at least she got it out of her system. Now she's just grateful you got in-school suspension instead of out-of-school. That way she *won't have to deal with you at home*.

Not like she deals with you that much anyway. She's always too busy with work.

The worst thing is that your brother's barely talking to you, either. Marshall's got more than one queer friend, and it doesn't bother you. It really doesn't. You're fine with all of them.

You don't hate gay people. You just . . .

You're not even sure what you were just, anymore. It feels like it was someone else who did it. Even though you remember saying it. You don't remember why. Or you do, but the reasons don't make sense now, not in the way they had before you did it. A pouch of Pop-Tarts doesn't seem to matter that much anymore.

Still, it was just one word. A word you'd never used before. Marshall knows you don't hate gay people. So why is he treating you like you do?

A rumble of thunder shakes the windowpanes. You didn't notice that it started raining. Now you can't even get out and go for a walk. Your mom always lets you or Marshall get out for exercise, even when you're grounded.

You can't even remember the last time you were grounded. Maybe sixth grade? You don't get in trouble. Not like this.

You roll over on your bed, fix the legs of your shorts where they're twisted and bunched around your thighs, and stare at the popcorn ceiling. Sometimes your dad talks about scraping it off to "increase the resale value." But so far it's still there, the texture smoothed by the soft gray light of a rainy day.

You were supposed to go to Sephora this afternoon, you and Cooper and Tyler. Tyler's mom was going to drive you. There's a sale on fragrances, clearing out the fall ones to make room for winter even though it's officially been fall for only a few days. Tyler's in it for the sale—at this point his bathroom is probably half bottles—but Cooper's still searching for a new signature scent.

"We're not boys anymore," he announced solemnly at his birthday party last weekend. "We're young men."

You haven't been able to talk to any of them since it all happened. You didn't even get to answer their texts before Dad confiscated your phone. But you picture them texting you now. Wondering what's up. Piling into Tyler's mom's car and driving to your house only to find out you can't come along.

You huff and roll out of bed.

"Where are you going?" Marshall asks as you walk past his open door. He's stretched out on his bed, scrolling on his phone. Your brother's got a good six inches in height on you, and his face is less round, but you still kind of look alike. Same hair, though he's started growing his out a bit. Same eyes. Same nose. Same smile, you think, though Marshall seems to get a lot more attention from girls for his than you do for yours. Which isn't fair, since you had the same orthodontist.

"I don't know," you admit. "I need to text the guys. We were supposed to go out today. But Mom and Dad still have my phone."

Marshall chuckles. "Good luck with that, then. You know what they're like."

You do.

No exceptions, that's Mom's rule. *Play stupid games, win stupid prizes*, that's Dad's.

"I know."

You sigh. God, maybe Dr. Matthews is rubbing off on you. Or maybe sighing is just a thing you do more of when you grow up.

"But the guys are probably on their way. I haven't even been able to tell them I'm grounded."

"They probably guessed," Marshall says, putting down his phone and crossing his arms. "You screwed up, bro. Big-time."

"I know. I'm sorry. What else do you want from me?"

Marshall just shakes his head. But you must look really pathetic, because his frown softens.

"Here. You've got two minutes. Don't look at my photos." He holds out his phone.

One, you're definitely not going to look at his photos, because, *gross*.

Two, you don't tell Marshall often enough, so: "I love you."

He scoffs as he hands you his phone, but you realize he doesn't have anyone's number. You switch over to Instagram and send Cooper a DM.

It's Dayton not Marshall

Can't make it today my dude

Grounded

You and the guys never called each other *dude* before. Much less *my dude*. But last week Tyler sent the group a meme of a bunch of forty-year-olds playing Roblox and calling one another *my dude* that had you all in stitches, so now you all use it ironically.

You wait for Cooper to answer. Maybe he doesn't recognize Marshall's account. But it's got Marshall's face as the profile pic, and Cooper's been at your house often enough to recognize your brother.

Maybe he and Tyler are already at Sephora. Maybe Cooper's already spritzing the little sampler wands and waving them, talking about top notes and woods versus florals. And Tyler's already pronouncing all the different names in a dramatic French accent.

Maybe Cooper's got his notifications muted. Or maybe he just doesn't have signal. It comes and goes in that Sephora.

But they wouldn't go to Sephora without you. Without at least checking on you.

Five seconds. Ten. Thirty.

Marshall raises his eyebrows, holds out his hand. You're about to give it back, but finally, finally, Cooper responds.

We figured.

That's all it says. Two words.

We figured.

You don't know what that means.

Somewhere in the house, a door opens and closes. Mom emerging from her midlife crisis home gym, probably. Marshall gestures for his phone back. But you want to hold on. Beg for more time. Ask Cooper what you missed and what people are saying. But surely that's all in the group chat. You'll be able to check whenever you get your phone back.

So you just send **Catch you Monday?** and hand Marshall his phone back.

"Thanks," you say.

"I'm still mad at you," Marshall says, wiping his screen against his T-shirt like you got germs on it.

"I didn't even do anything to you!"

"You hurt my friends, you hurt me," Marshall says. "And you haven't taken any accountability."

"What does that even mean?"

Before Marshall can answer, your mom calls from downstairs. "Dayton? You better not be goofing off."

"I'm not," you shout as you head back to your room. Flop onto your bed. Try not to feel so freaking lonely.

You'll catch up with your friends in school. Well, after school. It's not like they'll be in ISS with you.

Still, this will all blow over. It's not like you beat someone up or something. It was just one word.

Everything will be fine.

4

Farshid

THE VACUUM YOU'RE USING IS OLDER THAN YOU. IT'S LOUD, AND you have to push it hard, and one of the little lights on the front is burnt out. You imagine it winking at all the dust bunnies in the threadbare carpet of the Bahá'í Center's basement before devouring them like some scene from a horror movie.

Nour's obsessed with horror movies. Every time you hang out she's talking about some new one she's seen, trying to get you to watch it with her (even though she's already seen it twice), but that's a mistake you don't intend to make again.

One, it turns out you hate horror movies. You don't like blood, and you don't like gore, and you don't like jump scares, and you don't like music that makes you anxious, and you don't like the nightmares after, even though you don't admit to having them.

Two, even though Nour is quickly becoming an S-tier friend, she is a horrible person to watch a movie with, because she keeps a running commentary going whether you've seen the movie or not. Which is, if not fine, at least tolerable when it's just the two of you, because then her talking can distract you from being scared. But if you try to watch a movie with anyone else, they're usually less forgiving than you are.

There's no movies—horror or otherwise—for you this weekend.

For the past ten years (maybe longer, you honestly can't remember), your mom has been part of a group that helps clean the Bahá'í Center every Saturday, so they don't have to spend money on a cleaning service that doesn't always get the corners anyway.

And somehow, your mom being part of that group means you've been roped into it, too, you and your sister, Jina (and your brother, Nadeem, before he left for college), but you're the youngest so you got stuck vacuuming the basement while Maman and Jina are upstairs helping dust the furniture or cleaning the windows with a big squeegee, and both jobs are way better than dealing with this monstrosity of a vacuum with electrical tape wrapped around the cord in three different places.

Maybe if you get electrocuted you can get out of cleaning for a few weeks. You don't want to wind up in the hospital, but a little sympathy never hurt anyone.

The vacuum makes a weird crispy sound, and you turn it off to figure out if you just ran over something you shouldn't have, but the ringing silence lets you hear your mom's throaty voice calling you in Farsi.

"Farshid, are you almost done, maman?"

"Almost!" you yell back in English, but she comes down the stairs anyway, her pink tennis shoes squeaking softly against the hardwood stairs.

You have dim memories of her always wearing high heels everywhere when you first came here from Iran. Or maybe they're not your memories; maybe they're Nadeem's and Jina's memories and you've just heard them often enough they feel like yours. You were three years old when you moved, and you don't remember much from that time, but you think you remember a few things. Your first time playing in the snow, chasing your siblings around the tiny stretch of grass between the parking lot and the doors of your first apartment. It was in North Kansas City, just off the highway, and Maman and Baba still point it out every time you drive into downtown, even though you can't see the complex from the highway because of all the trees in the way.

You keep the vacuum off as Maman comes up and pinches at the shoulder seam of your Magic: The Gathering T-shirt.

"We need to get you more shirts," she says. "You keep growing."

You shrug. You're taller than Nadeem now, even though he's three years older than you, a fact that annoys him greatly, but at least he stopped picking fights with you. The moment he realized you'd gotten as big as him—that you could hit back as strong as he could—you both kind of just stopped.

You're glad for that, at least.

"Are you doing okay?" Maman asks you, brown eyes crinkling with concern, though her forehead doesn't wrinkle up. She got her monthly Botox last week, so her forehead is always worry-free, no matter what's going on in your life, or hers for that matter. Including the email from your principal, which she called a family meeting over last night, to make sure you all still felt *safe* in your school.

But safety's all relative, at least here in America, where strangers can come and shoot you in class. As opposed to back in Iran, where the police could come and kidnap you from class, and then kill you later in secret.

"I'm fine, Maman," you remind her. "I've just got one more corner to do."

"I meant with school," she said. "You're not getting bullied?"

She can't know about what people are saying behind your back, can she? The principal didn't go into details about the incident, and you're not 100 percent certain your mom knows *that* word in English anyway.

"I'm good. Really."

She purses her lips. Those, at least, are still natural, you're pretty sure, because they have little lines in the corners that show when she smiles or frowns or sips her tea. They're painted a dark red that pops against her sienna skin.

"You know you can talk to me anytime, right? About anything?"

"I know," you lie, because you remember last year when Jina announced she had a boyfriend, and your mom removed Jina's door from the frame. She put it back thirty minutes later, but still. *Overprotective* doesn't begin to describe it.

"Okay." She pulls your head down to kiss your forehead. "There's lunch upstairs when you're finished. Khanum Kermani brought dolmeh."

You do love Khanum Kermani's dolmeh, steamed grape leaves stuffed with meat and rice and golden raisins. You could probably eat an entire batch by yourself.

"I'll be right up," you promise.

Your mom retreats up the stairs, her shoes squeak-squeak-squeaking again, the wooden steps creak-creak-creaking, and you finally breathe, because no, you're not going to talk to your mom about it.

Telling Maman what your classmates are saying in the halls—maybe even what they're calling you, you can't be sure—means telling her what it means, and telling her what it means would lead to questions you really don't want to have to answer.

Not yet. In fact, not ever.

5

DAYTON

YOU'VE NEVER BEEN SUSPENDED BEFORE, IN SCHOOL OR OUT.

You've never even gotten detention.

The worst trouble you've ever been in was that one time in fourth grade where you collided with this girl—you can't even remember her name anymore—and you both got demerits for playing too rough at recess.

You don't even know where the ISS room is. You go to the attendance office and the admin, who you never talk to because you've never needed to before, doesn't even look up from her computer as she tells you where to go.

You're almost late. You didn't know Meadowbrook *had* a G Hall: a short cross hall connecting the E and F Halls down past both gyms. You open the door and step inside right as the bell rings.

For a second you think you're in the wrong place. This isn't a classroom. This is a broom closet.

Not literally—there aren't any brooms or mops or whatever—but it's tiny. Four desks, though they look more like cubicles, against the far wall; two more at the corner, making an L shape. There aren't any windows, just the usual "motivational" posters that look like they've been hanging since last century. There's one teacher's desk but no teacher behind it. No one else is here.

You're about to back out and keep looking when the door opens again, bumping your backpack and shoving you forward.

"Sorry, man," a voice says. It's low, but kind of pinched. "You have to sign in."

"Huh?" You correct yourself. Your mom's always on you to *speak properly*. "What?"

You turn and find the voice's owner. He's in your conditioning class, but you don't remember his name. He's always at the far end of the gym during warm-ups, and you've never been teamed up with him for anything.

He's white but super tanned, and stocky, built like he should be on a farm in central Missouri instead of here in the suburbs of Kansas City. His black hair is cropped short, like someone did it with clippers. His brown eyes are deep-set above a long, triangular nose.

"The sign-in sheet." He points to a clipboard on the teacher's desk, and sure enough, there's a lined paper, but the string attached to the clipboard doesn't have a pencil at the other end.

"I got you." He pulls out a mechanical pencil, clicks it ostentatiously, moves in front of you to sign, then hands the pencil over to you. He's in bright yellow gym shorts and a black tee with the logo of some band you don't recognize. You're not sure if those are supposed to be bull horns or devil horns. You're too nervous to ask.

"Thanks." You sign your name—*Dayton Reilly*—right below his. *Brody Connors, frosh*.

You add *9th grade* to yours, too.

Brody goes to take a desk, and you move to take the one next to him, but he stops you.

"No homo, but bathroom rules apply here."

You blink at him. What are bathroom rules?

"You know, skip a spot. You don't pee right next to someone, do you?"

"Oh. Yeah. I mean, no. Duh."

So you skip a desk and take the next. Brody pulls a folder out of his backpack and flops it onto the desk. His chair's metal legs screech against the floor as he sits.

You copy him, but you don't have a folder. You don't know what you're supposed to do.

"First time here?" he asks when he notices you looking.

"They didn't give me a folder or anything."

"Ms. Anderson will be here sooner or later. She can show you the ropes." He angles himself to sort of lean against the wall of his cubicle. "What'd you do to land in here anyway?"

Your face flushes, and you hate when that happens, because *everyone* can tell with your pasty complexion.

"Disrupted the assembly last Friday," you say.

Brody's eyes go wide. "That was you?"

You nod. Brody must've heard. Or seen the email that went out. But that email didn't have the whole story, so you tell him yourself.

"And you didn't even get your twenty dollars?" he asks when you finish. "That's cold."

You shrug. "I haven't even seen Reggie since then."

Brody rolls his eyes. "No surprise. Reggie thinks he's better than everyone."

"Maybe." He's not exactly your friend. You only met him this year, when you got seated next to each other in ELA. But maybe Brody's right.

You crack a tiny grin.

"Seriously, though, that's kind of epic," Brody says. "You're gonna be a legend."

You don't want to be a legend. You just want to survive freshman year. Pass your classes. That kind of stuff. Maybe get a girlfriend? You're not 100 percent sure on that just yet.

But you definitely don't want to be the guy everyone thinks goes around shouting slurs at strangers, like some sort of . . . walking hate crime or something.

It wasn't even a crime. And you don't hate anyone.

It was just a word. A word you shouted because you weren't thinking.

You don't know how to explain that to Brody, though. Especially since he finds the whole thing funny. He makes it feel less serious. Less like the world has ended.

You didn't know how much you needed that.

"What about you?" You mirror his lean against your own cubicle, but the walls are flimsier than you thought, and you nearly topple over when it fails to hold your weight.

"Careful," Brody says, lunging forward to grab your knee before your chair tips. He releases you with another "No homo."

"Thanks." You didn't think it was homo. But anyway. "So? What'd you do?"

Brody rolls his eyes again. They're big and brown and expressive, but the shadow of his heavy brow makes them look a little mischievous, too. "Ah, nothing as good as yours." He sighs and rests his hands behind his head. "Ms. Wilson heard me and Chris joking about whacking it. Well, she heard *me* joking about *him* doing it too much, so he got off scot-free and I got ISS."

He blows a raspberry.

"Three days, same as you. And no offense, but how is that fair? I didn't even offend anyone."

"Yeah. That sucks," you agree, though your insides squirm.

Brody and Chris aren't the only guys who joke about that kind of stuff. Everyone's making jokes and hand motions whenever the teachers aren't around. You don't remember that being a thing, back in eighth grade. Well, except for that rumor about Bentley Morris doing it at the back of the bus on the way home from a field trip to the Nelson-Atkins. But you don't think that was true.

Still, Bentley isn't here this year. He transferred to a private high school.

"Right? Everybody does it," Brody says. "It's not like . . . sexual harassment or something."

You don't do it. Should you be?

You don't even know how. You've touched yourself, sure, but nothing really . . . happened. Maybe you're doing it wrong, but there's no one you can ask, not your parents and *definitely* not Marshall, who would never let you hear the end of it. Though now you think about it, he did start spending a lot longer in the shower back when he first started high school. You snicker.

"Yeah, my older brother likes to take long showers these days."

Brody laughs, a wild, free sound that eases the tightness in your stomach. It's not from hunger or anything: Your mom and dad finally got groceries this weekend, so you managed to grab a granola bar before school. But the ISS room makes you feel . . . weird.

Trapped.

Brody's laughter makes you feel better.

"You get me," he says. "We're guys. It's not a big deal."

Somehow it feels like one. You're not sure why.

Brody laughs again, and you find yourself laughing, too, because he's right, you are just guys.

You're still laughing when the door opens and Ms. Anderson walks in, holding a stuffed folder.

"No talking," she says automatically, even though you and Brody both went silent as soon as she came in. "Face forward, please. Dayton, this is the work you're missing today. Be sure to stop by the main office tomorrow morning to get your new one. You'll do that every day you're here."

Three days. It's only three days.

You won't be here again after that.

You're not a bad kid.

But then, Brody doesn't seem that bad, either. Maybe he jokes a little too much, but he's harmless. So maybe ISS isn't for bad kids. Maybe it's just for whoever they've decided to punish that day.

And for the next three days, that's you.

So you nod and take your work. There's no making up the rehearsal you're missing in choir, so you pull out your English homework.

A reflection on last Friday's talk. That you missed most of.

Great.

6

Farshid

YOU THINK YOU HEAR IT IN THE HALLS AGAIN, BUT YOU CAN'T BE sure. The hallways are noisy—friends laughing, teachers hurrying by, locker doors slamming, shoes squeaking—so maybe you heard it again, or maybe someone was talking about Dayton Reilly, or maybe you're just becoming paranoid.

You don't think you're gay anyway. You really don't. So it doesn't matter, does it? Then again, who you really are has never mattered to your classmates nearly as much as who they think you are.

You got your citizenship when you were eight years old. You still remember Maman and Baba taking the Oath of Allegiance, and even though you and Jina and Nadeem were too young, the judge let you pledge allegiance to the flag so you could still feel like a part of everything.

You were so excited you kept practicing it around the house, pledging allegiance to the Persian rugs on the floor, the quilts hanging over the couch, the crayon drawing of a flag with the wrong number of stars and stripes you'd done in kindergarten.

And you pledged allegiance every morning in school, too, even though the teachers said it was optional. At least up until middle school, when suddenly it stopped, and instead of the Pledge of

Allegiance there were morning announcements, but that's okay because by then Nadeem was in high school and had decided America wasn't so great after all. Better than Iran, to be sure, but far from perfect, and maybe pledging allegiance to the flag painted on all the bombs that had been falling on people that looked like you for so many decades wasn't cool after all.

And now there aren't morning announcements at all. Instead there's *Meadowbrook News*, every lunchtime, and you kind of want to sign up for journalism next year because you think you'd be way better at designing the graphics for the news segments than whoever is doing it this year and keeps picking D-tier fonts like Papyrus for everything.

You stuff your bio homework into your locker—despite Jina's constant warnings, you haven't dissected a frog yet, and hopefully you never will—and grab your history stuff. Your grade still isn't up on the portal, a fact that Maman nagged you about this morning, like it was your fault it takes a while to grade a hundred quizzes, or like you skipped school and she just hasn't found out yet.

You don't know why she's in your business so much these days.

You close your locker and turn to go, but then you hear it.

One word. Six letters.

Someone said it.

Someone definitely said it.

You whip around, but no one is looking at you. Everyone is acting like nothing is wrong, except you can see cheeks puffed out with suppressed laughter, teeth biting lips, hear a snort, a giggle, spot some sophomore slapping another kid's shoulder, and no one is looking at you. You can't tell who's not looking because you're an invisible freshman and who's not looking because they're deliberately avoiding it. Because they think you're a . . . that. Or because maybe they don't think you are but they think it's funny when you get called that, or because they're the one who said it but they don't want to get caught and sent to the office if you tell someone.

Your face feels hot, prickly, though your skin is still summer-dark, brown enough to hide most blushes, so they won't see your humiliation.

Harder to hide is the burning in your eyes that makes you blink even though you don't want to. If they know they're getting to you, they'll only do it worse.

Don't react.

Back in sixth grade, someone Scotch-taped a KICK ME sign to your backpack, and you thought that was just a thing in TV shows, but people actually did it, your own classmates, though you never knew who, you only knew that first you thought someone had bumped into you but then *everyone* was bumping into you—not bumping, kicking you in the rear—and you didn't know *why* until you got to science and took your backpack off and saw the note, and your teacher saw you crying and asked what was wrong, and he saw the note, but no one ever got in trouble. No one knew who started it. No one saw who did it.

It was just all around you, and crying only made it worse, because then you were a sixth-grade crybaby.

So you don't cry and you don't let anyone know they're bothering you. You clutch your backpack straps over your tightening chest as you blend into the stream of students and hope no one sees you, recognizes you, knows you exist at all.

Invisible.

High school was supposed to be *better* than middle school. Not more of the same.

YOUR MOM INSISTS ON PICKING YOU UP FROM SCHOOL EVERY DAY, even though you could easily ride the bus.

You and Jina wait in the pickup line. Well, you wait, and Jina talks to her friends and acts like you don't exist, even though you'll both have to get into the car together when Maman shows up in her minivan.

Your underarms are sweaty from conditioning, where you spent the whole class running laps on the field in the sun, and you're glad you have it seventh hour so you can go home and shower right after and not have to sit through class worrying that you smell bad.

You're even more glad you don't have to shower at school. You were scared that was really a thing, because you see it on TV sometimes, like schools are just full of showers. You think you'd rather die than have to shower with any of your classmates around.

A voice calls your name, your real name, and you glance over your shoulder but turn back quick.

It's Dayton.

Dayton, who spent the day in ISS. Dayton, who had an email sent out to the whole school and parents and community about him. Dayton, who hates gay people.

Why else would he have shouted what he did at the top of his lungs, shouted at a guest who literally got you out of class, and all you had to do was sit and listen to a talk about poetry?

He could've even taken a nap.

But no, he decided to shout that word at the top of his lungs.

Does Dayton think *you're* gay?

You're not. You really don't think you are.

Then again, you're not Muslim, either, and that hasn't stopped people making assumptions.

Dayton calls your name again, but thankfully you spot the pale blue of Maman's minivan pulling into the drive, and you run for it.

Dayton might not have called you anything to your face, but he's just as bad as the kids saying it in the halls. Maybe worse.

At least they're too ashamed to show their faces.

Dayton showed his to the whole school.

You get in the middle row of the minivan, even though your legs are longer, because Jina always wants the front, and you don't have time to argue with her today, not if you're going to get in the car in time to make your escape. You push the button and the door slides closed so agonizingly slowly, you want to yank it closed yourself, but doing that messes up the motor.

"Hi, maman," your mom says, then switches to Farsi. "How was school?"

"Fine," you answer in English, staring back through the safety of the tinted window. Dayton's still out there, talking to someone you recognize. Brody Connors. He's in a pair of yellow gym shorts that are tight around his thighs, no doubt to show off his gains. You don't get it. Even when you ask Nadeem to help you lift weights in the gym down the block from the Bahá'í Center, your legs never look like that. Maybe you have bad leg genetics.

Brody's legs fill out his shorts. He's probably been doing squats or something. He looks athletic and strong. He looks . . .

God, what if they're right about you?

But they're not. They're not. You just need to be more dedicated.

Maybe find a gym that's closer so you can go every day. Get a more reliable trainer than Nadeem, who drives home from Lawrence only once a week.

"Farshid? Farshid? Hello?" your mom asks in English.

"What?"

"Did you hear about your test?"

"No! I told you I'd tell you. Can you just drop it?"

Why is she so hung up on your quiz anyway? You told her you passed it. You told her the grade would be posted. She can log in to the portal just as easily as you can.

Why is she on your case?

Your mom goes quiet, listening to Jina complain about her trigonometry class, and faces forward as the line finally starts to move. You're not sure why you snapped at her like that. She always worries about your grades. She always worries about everything. You should be used to it by now.

You don't feel guilty for how you acted. She needs to learn to back off.

You're fourteen now.

She can't keep treating you like a child.

7

DAYTON

YOU WATCH FARSHID PRACTICALLY THROW HIMSELF INTO HIS mom's car when you call his name. You loaned him a pencil just last week. He let you borrow his notes. You've never had a problem with him, and he's never had a problem with you.

All you wanted was to ask a question about your assignment in US history. He sits right in front of you. Now he's avoiding you.

You thought, or maybe hoped, that people would forget about you over the weekend. Or at least have moved on. Now would be a great time for someone to go through a messy breakup in the middle of the cafeteria. Or start a fight in the halls. Or vandalize a teacher's car.

Anything to get the attention off you.

ISS was quiet, and boring, except for the times when Ms. Anderson stepped out and you and Brody could talk a little. He's a funny guy, Brody. You're not glad to be in ISS, but you're glad he's there with you, because it doesn't feel so bad being punished if there's a friend with you.

Brody feels like a friend, even though you've only known him for one day. But seven hours spent hunched over a cubicle desk, quietly scratching away at your work, can bond two guys quicker than just about anything.

Not that you spent all seven hours actually working. There wasn't actually seven hours' worth of work. Most of it wasn't that hard. Even the history worksheet wasn't hard, you just wanted to ask Farshid what he put down for question ten.

When you finished your work, Ms. Anderson let you pick a book from the small shelf in the corner, but all the books were old and beaten up and written before you were born, not new ones like Mr. Clemens keeps on one wall of his classroom, crisp new paperbacks with the spines still unbroken and the pages clean and unfolded. Not to mention they were all written this century.

Still, you picked up a book about some rich kid finding ways to still have problems at boarding school. It was so boring you skimmed ahead and found out this guy basically shoved his friend out of a tree, and then the friend died. So what are you supposed to take away from that, anyway?

You already felt like crap, and the book just made you feel crappier.

"You good?" Brody snaps you out of it. He's standing next to you, squinting in the sunlight. After all that time in the windowless ISS room, it's way too bright.

"I'm good." You are. ISS sucks, but making a new friend kind of makes up for that. "Thanks."

"Sure, bro. I gotta catch the bus. See you tomorrow?" He holds out a hand; you clasp and go for a bro hug. He claps you once on the shoulder and gives you a grin.

"See you." You watch him go, picking at the cuticle on your left middle finger, which is doing that annoying thing where it sticks up. Normally you'd take the bus—or ride home with Marshall, if he doesn't have practice after school—but today you have to wait for your dad to pick you up. He and Mom are convinced you'd try to get around your grounding if you took the bus. What do they think you'd do? Get off at the wrong stop? Go egg a house?

You spot Cooper coming out of the side door by the science wing, and you wave at him, but he doesn't see you. You scan the line, but there's still no sign of your dad, so you jog over.

"Hey! Coop!"

He finally looks your way.

"Oh. Hey." He stuffs his hands in his pockets. "What's up?"

"Nothing." You shrug. Your backpack smacks your lower back. "You?"

"Not much." He bites his lip and looks around you, past you.

"How was Sephora? Find anything good?"

"A couple things."

You wait for him to say more, but he's still not looking at you.

"Everything all right?" you ask.

When he finally does look at you, there's something in his eyes that makes your stomach do a backflip.

"You really have to ask?"

He sounds angry.

He *is* angry.

At you.

"What's that supposed to mean?" you ask. "I told you I couldn't make it—"

"It's not about you being grounded and missing Sephora, *my dude*," Cooper says, but when he says *my dude* it's more sarcastic than ironic. "It's about why you were grounded."

"Come on, man, you know I didn't mean anything by it. I wasn't thinking, and Reggie bet me twenty bucks, and—"

"You don't use a word like that without meaning it," Cooper says. "That's messed up."

Your jaw is clenching up. You *didn't* mean it.

You didn't!

"It was just a joke." How many times do you have to explain yourself? Like no one's ever told a bad joke before. "I'm sorry."

"Me too," he says. "I'm sorry I have to explain to everyone I know that I'm not a homophobe just because I used to be friends with you."

Your throat turns to sandpaper. "Used to be?"

"You know I got like a five-minute lecture from Mr. Cain the other day, just to make sure I would *behave myself* because my stand mate is trans?"

Cooper plays second violin in the orchestra. He's really good. He's been playing since fifth grade.

"I didn't mean it," you say again. "It's not like I said—"

You don't finish that sentence, though, because even as the words tumble out of your mouth you know they're messed up. Cooper knows, too. His lower lip trembles. He runs a hand over his fade.

You've never said *that* word (*r* or no *r*), not even when Cooper did as you sang along to Lil Nas X. Cooper's allowed to and you're not. It's not like you even want to say that word. You've *never* wanted to. Never even thought about it. You're not racist.

And you're not a homophobe, either.

"I didn't mean it," you say again, because what else is there? "It was a mistake."

"I thought I knew you," Cooper says, and your stomach drops into your feet when he blinks and a teardrop sparkles in the corner of his eye.

He does know you, better than your own family. You've been friends since forever.

You try to say something, anything, but your voice doesn't work. You don't think you've ever made Cooper cry before.

"I can't be around you," he says, soft but final, and then he's moving past you. Away from you. Trailing some new woodsy, smoky fragrance he must've found at Sephora with Tyler. Without you.

You and Cooper went to kindergarten together.

You've been to his house more times than you can count.

He was the one you told when you got a crush on Julia Vostock back in seventh grade.

You were the one who went with him to his grandpa's funeral.

And now it's all gone?

Just like that?

Maybe your friendship wasn't as strong as you thought, if he can throw it all away over one single word.

One word that doesn't even affect him.

One word you didn't even mean.

Your throat tightens. Your stomach churns. Not with nerves but with anger. How can Cooper just drop you like that? Not even give you a chance to explain?

You've only known Brody for a day, and he was cooler about this whole thing than your best friend in the whole world.

Former best friend.

Screw him anyway.

BRODY'S WITH YOU YOUR SECOND DAY OF ISS, BUT YOUR THIRD DAY, he goes back to class, leaving you alone. And bored. Now it's just you, the awkward silence stretching between you and Ms. Anderson as she types away on her computer, answering emails or writing reports or doing spreadsheets or whatever it is teachers do when they're not teaching.

But today, when you finish your work and get up to find another boring old book to read, she stops you.

"Huh?" You flinch, imagining your mom correcting you again. "Sorry, what?"

"I'd like you to do one more thing today," she says. That might be the longest sentence she's said to you. Mostly it's just been variations of "No talking."

"Okay?"

She pulls out a piece of paper with the Meadowbrook logo (a forest-green cougar) in the corner.

"Dr. Matthews thought you might like the opportunity to write an apology to Mr. Markham."

"Oh." There's that clenching in your stomach again, the hot shame you've gotten so familiar with the past few days. It stews in your gut. At least, it does when you're not busy being mad at Cooper and Tyler. Betrayal doesn't even begin to cover it.

But Mr. Markham didn't do anything to you. You did something to him. You know it was messed up. And if you can say sorry to him, at least that will solve one of your problems. You can take accountability, like Marshall said.

And then things can go back to normal. Your friends will forgive you. People will stop avoiding you in the halls. You can start taking the bus again.

"Yeah. Okay."

Except when you sit and click your pencil, you realize the last piece of lead is shattered, and you don't have any refills. You turn; Ms. Anderson notices and raises an eyebrow.

"My pencil's empty," you say sheepishly.

You think she might be trying not to laugh at you. But she hands you a nonmechanical pencil, round and blunt at the tip and with barely any eraser left. You get up to sharpen it, then sit back down.

DEAR MR. MARKHAM, you write.

And then you stare at the paper. It's one thing to say you're sorry, but another to write a whole letter about it. There's all that blank space, and *I'm sorry* is only two words. One more word than the thing that got you into this whole mess.

And it's not like he cares anyway, right? He doesn't live here. He's off in California with all the other fancy people with expensive haircuts and spray tans and fake white teeth and tight pants.

He'll never see you again. So what does it matter?

You almost crumple up the paper. Rip it into pieces and toss it in the trash. You're sorry, but do you have to spend the rest of your life being sorry? You're not the only person in the world who ever made a mistake.

You almost give up. But something stops you.

Maybe it's the look Marshall keeps giving you over the kitchen table. Or the way Cooper's lip trembled as he broke off a decade of friendship with you. Or the fact Reggie never did give you that twenty dollars.

It was just a joke. You didn't mean it. But still, it was wrong.

So you pick up your pencil.

MY NAME IS DAYTON REILLY, AND I WANTED TO WRITE SO I COULD APOLOGIZE TO YOU FOR WHAT HAPPENED AT YOUR VISIT . . .

YOU'RE RELIEVED THAT BRODY'S WAITING FOR YOU AT THE PICKUP line.

You weren't sure if you were really going to become friends, or if you were just friendly because you were stuck together.

But he smiles when he sees you.

"Look who's finally made parole." He reaches out to clasp your hand and bro-hug you. He just came from seventh-period conditioning. His forehead and hairline are damp with sweat, and his T-shirt clings to his neck.

"Look who needs a shower," you joke back, and then wish you hadn't, because what if he thinks you mean it?

But he cracks a grin and laughs. "Don't act so superior. You'll be back with us tomorrow, won't you?"

You nod.

"Good. I better go." He gestures to his bus. "See you?"

"Yeah. Tomorrow."

He walks backward, giving you a funny salute before spinning around and running for the bus, arms flailing.

You laugh.

Yeah, the week has sucked so far. And yeah, you wish you could go back and not do what you did.

But you like Brody. He gets you. And being his friend takes the sting out of everything.

You breathe a little easier as you grip the straps of your backpack and wait for your dad.

PART 2

november

8

FARSHID

AT BREAKFAST, YOUR FATHER SITS AT THE TABLE RIGHT NEXT TO you, not in his usual spot closest to the coffeepot. That's if he even sits at all; most days, he fills his thermos, wishes you and Jina a good day, kisses Maman, and heads for the garage.

But today Baba drops into the chair next to you as you eat your scrambled eggs. They're a bit rubbery; you still tend to overcook them. Maman thinks you have the heat too high, but you don't need them to be fluffy and perfect, you need them to be high in protein, which they are, whether they're golden clouds or burnt yellow pebbles.

Baba's hair has started thinning in the back lately, and he seems to have decided to offset it by growing a beard, which you can't remember him ever doing before. He's losing his summer tan, you both are, desert-brown skin fading to a lighter shade of earth.

"Farshid," he says, like he's pronouncing judgment on you, but you haven't done anything wrong recently, other than the fact you keep fighting with your mom. You haven't done much of anything except school, and homework, and the new gym you begged Baba to sign you up for, a boxing-gym franchise that's a mile away, so you can jog to it every day.

He seems to realize he sounds too serious, too, because he

clears his throat and tries again. "You're growing up, baba," he says.

Please, please don't let this be another *talk*.

You don't know if you can survive another one. The last one, after he noticed you'd left the lotion on the sink counter instead of its usual spot in the cabinet, was enough to make you want to throw yourself into the Missouri River.

"Yeah?" you ask, shoveling another forkful of eggs into your mouth. You've still got to shower before school.

He nods and sets a plastic Target bag on the table.

"Your mom and I want you to feel confident," he says, switching to Farsi. You've noticed he does that whenever he's uncomfortable with the subject. "So we got you this."

Please, please, please . . .

You don't know what it is you're dreading, exactly, but thankfully it's not that.

What it *is* is an electric razor.

Your ears start to tingle as you stare at it.

"It's time you started grooming. If you want to. But your mustache is getting . . ."

He hesitates.

The Persian language is one of poetry, of metaphor, of obliquely saying what you mean. But apparently even the language of Rumi and Hafez is failing Baba, who finally switches back to English. "Scruffy."

You drop your fork and reach for your upper lip. The hair up there has been getting darker, you suppose, but not, like, a *mustache*. It's just peach fuzz. From a slightly darker peach.

"It's your choice," he says, reaching over to ruffle your hair, but he stops himself, because it's damp from your morning workout. You hate getting up at five in the morning for the early class, but you like being able to get eight rounds in before school, and making it home with enough time to eat and shower. Then you can go back after school, catch another class, lift weights, and run home for dinner.

Baba pats his thighs and stands. "I've got to get to work. Love you, baba."

"Love you," you say as he leaves. You shovel the rest of your eggs into your mouth, stick your plate in the dishwasher, and run to the bathroom, which Jina has thankfully vacated.

You stare at your face in the mirror. You didn't think it was that obvious, but now, you can't help noticing how uneven all the hairs are, some longer, some shorter, some darker, some lighter, denser in some places than others. You *do* look scruffy. And though you're getting some gains in your legs from all the squats—they're solidly B-tier now—your arms are still too gangly, and your shoulders haven't broadened like you want them to, despite all the boxing and the protein shakes and the eggs every morning.

It turns out you should've been more worried about your upper body genetics than your lower body, but you're doing your best to compensate.

You've also got a fresh pimple coming in on your chin, plus an old one healing on your nose.

You fight the packaging and finally get the razor out. Three silver discs, clustered together at one end, hum to life when you hit the power button. You look for instructions, but they only say how to turn the thing on and off, how to charge it and clean it, let you know it's waterproof but shouldn't be submerged in water, remind you that water and electricity don't mix.

There's nothing on how to actually *shave*.

Isn't your father supposed to teach you or something?

You'd look up a video on YouTube, but your phone is charging in your room.

So you do your best.

"FARSHID, YOU NEED YOUR COAT," YOUR MOM SAYS AS YOU PULL UP at the drop-off.

"I have one!" It's stuffed into your backpack.

"It's cold out. Why are you still wearing shorts?"

"It's not that cold." It's still above freezing, and anyway, your legs are the only things worth showing off. Your sweatshirt hides the lack of growth in your D-tier arms and C-tier shoulders, and keeps you plenty warm. "Would you just let it go?"

"I'm only trying—"

"Trying to control me!" you spit. "I'm fine. God. Just let me go to class."

You unbuckle your seat belt and wait impatiently for the door to slide open, swinging out as soon as the gap is wide enough, except it's not quite wide enough and your backpack snags for a moment, so you yank harder, ignoring Maman calling after you to have a good day. You would, if she'd stop smothering you.

Your face feels weird and raw, your upper lip still burning, stinging at the gust of cold air that bites you on the way to the doors.

Nour beats you to first hour, and she gestures impatiently for you to take your seat behind her. She spins around, drumming her green fingernails against the red plastic of the chair attached to her desk, while you pull out your notebook. Her keffiyeh looks cozy where it lays across her shoulders, and for a second you regret how you talked to your mother as you got out of the car, because it *was* cold this morning, and your shorts and boxers let the cold air go right up to your core, but no way are you going back to the tighty-whities Maman used to buy for you back in middle school, even though they did keep you warmer and even though they did do a better job hiding the occasional accidental *excitement*.

But your sweatshirt's long enough to pull down past your waist, should the worst *arise*.

"What are you doing after school?" she asks without preamble.

"Going to the gym, why?"

"Come to RC with me."

"RC . . ." Your eyebrows bunch up as you try to figure out what she's talking about. "Rainbow Coalition?"

Rainbow Coalition is the renamed Gender and Sexuality Alliance, which was the renamed Queer Student Association, which was the renamed Gay-Straight Alliance. You wonder what it'll be named by the time you finally graduate.

And then you wonder why Nour suddenly wants to go.

Oh God. Is she coming out to you? You're honored she trusts you enough, and a little worried for her if you're honest, because only two months ago Dayton Reilly shouted a slur in front of the entire freshman class and all he got was three days of ISS, and Nour is already conspicuously brown, so adding any kind of queerness to it would just paint a bigger target on her back.

But you're also happy for her, and proud of her bravery, and you're getting ready to tell her so when she rolls her eyes, cutting you off.

"I'm going as an ally. For Esperanza."

Esperanza is one of Nour's best friends, though she's a sophomore, so you don't hang out that much.

"Oh. Cool." You didn't know that about Esperanza.

"So? Will you come? She says they need more allies."

You want to say no.

You want to tell her you heard that word in the cafeteria just last week, that Dayton and Brody still look at you funny in the locker room, that you don't want people to talk about you any more than they already do, that it's not worth the risk, that you're too busy anyway because despite the increased protein intake and heavier weights and larger sets you're still not seeing the changes you want in your body composition.

But this is Nour you're talking to, and she doesn't take no for an answer, not when she's right, and she is right. You should be an ally.

You can't let the Daytons and Brodys of the world win.

"Okay."

AFTER CONDITIONING, YOU SWIPE EXTRA DEODORANT UNDER YOUR shaking arms, snap your locker shut, and hurry out of the locker room, avoiding the wrestling team pouring in to get changed for their practice. You almost want to wait and see what their workouts are like, because some of them have really impressive shoulders, but you're worried they'd take it the wrong way, and anyway, you promised Nour.

So you fight the tide back across school to the library, where RC meets in one of the smaller rooms next to the café.

You get two cups of hot water, one for you and one for Nour, because one thing your mom does that *doesn't* annoy you these days is fill your backpack with bags of Persian tea, "just in case." So you hand Nour a cup of steaming tea and cradle your own and swallow your dread as you follow her inside.

The room is already full of students from every year, plus Mx. Lee, your biology teacher. Everyone's talking and milling about, and Nour is quick to abandon you to go talk to Esperanza. It's so packed, you're almost afraid to enter, afraid that the room might pop like that pimple on your chin. But it's a strange relief, too, that so many people are here. You don't know why, you really don't, but it makes you happy.

"First time here?" a soft voice asks as you hover near the door, still a bit afraid to press into the throng. You turn, almost spilling your tea, and find Cooper Norton. He's in orchestra with you, second violin, but you've never really talked to him since he sits so far away from you. The light streaming in through the glass blocks highlights his sharp cheekbones, the rich brown of his skin, the pink of his lips. All the girls in your class like to talk about how hot he is, and you suppose he is kind of good-looking, with a broad, earnest smile. He wears a soft-looking green Meadowbrook sweatshirt, and he smells like almond and vanilla and sweet smoke from a summer fire when you're making s'mores.

You wonder why he's here, if he's an ally or if he's queer or some secret third thing.

"Farshid?" he asks again, and you're surprised when he nearly pronounces it correctly.

"Hm? Yeah. It's my first time." You swallow, expecting him to ask if you're gay, and you definitely don't think you are. You're just here to support a friend. Well, a friend of a friend.

But instead he says, "Welcome. There's cookies."

He gestures toward a table in the corner, and there *are* cookies, but they're a bunch of sugar and you're avoiding refined sugars right now. If they had some fresh fruit or nuts or something, that would be a different story.

You're surprised to see Cooper here. You thought he was friends with Dayton. The two of them (and Tyler) used to cluster together in the halls, or take up half a table in the cafeteria, or wait for the bus together after school. But maybe they're not friends anymore. If Cooper's here, that means he doesn't hate gay people the way Dayton does.

A little knot inside your chest untangles itself, and you manage to smile, a little one because your upper lip still feels weird and kind of burnt from trying to shave this morning. You wonder if Cooper has to shave.

"Farshid?"

"Huh?"

"Cookies?"

"Oh. No thanks. I'm good."

9

DAYTON

"WHAT ABOUT THIS ONE?" YOU ASK, OFFERING BRODY A SAMPLER stick with the new CK on it.

Brody sniffs and shrugs. "I don't know. They all smell the same."

You don't let your shoulders slump. You don't.

Brody really isn't into fragrance. He didn't have to go with you to pick something new out for winter. But he's a good friend.

"I'm sure whatever will be fine," he adds, though his eyes slide past yours toward the corner where you know a couple of girls from your school—juniors or seniors—are looking at the makeup. He subtly straightens his posture and rolls back his shoulders to emphasize his chest. Even with the November frost, he's still in a T-shirt.

You're in an ugly sweater your dad got at his work Christmas party last year. It's hideous—gray and brown and purple, the weirdest combination of colors, and a psychedelic pattern that looks straight out of the 1960s—but it made you laugh, and it's warm and cozy. Your dad let you have it since he was never going to wear it.

You put back the CK and pick up another bottle. You don't recognize it, but something about it is calling your name. It's wrapped in orange-brown leather, and the label reads Vince Camuto. You've never heard of him, but you spritz another sampler stick and waft a bit your way. It's . . . spicy. Woodsy, you think, with top notes of . . . hm.

You're not as good at this as Cooper was, or Tyler. You haven't spoken to the boys in weeks. Cooper wasn't the only one who ditched you: Tyler did, too. Like you were toxic. Like you were nothing. Like you were a *bad kid*.

You did your punishment. You wrote your apology. You took accountability. But that wasn't enough for them. Nothing was.

Thank god for Brody. You lost two friends, but you gained a best friend. You might be invisible to the rest of the school, but Brody sees you. Brody gets you.

He just doesn't get fragrance.

"Sorry. I'm almost done."

"It's cool. I don't get it, but you like it," Brody says as you put the Camuto back and pick up a square blue bottle of Versace. You can't afford it, but you and the guys always used to smell it anyway, just to feel fancy.

"I like smelling good," you say with a shrug.

Brody's your best friend, but you can't tell him—can't tell anyone—about that awkward conversation with your piano teacher. You were twelve years old, and she told you that you were becoming a man and needed to start wearing deodorant, because it was winter and too cold to air out her practice studio between lessons.

So you like knowing for sure that you smell good. And you like it when girls compliment you on your scent.

Last week Mariana Herrera, this girl in German, leaned over and sniffed your collar like she couldn't help herself, and it excited you so much you had to keep your hands in your lap, so you missed placing your chips for BINGO (or LOTTO, as Frau calls it). Which sucked, because Frau was giving out real German chocolate to whoever won, which would've been an epic Halloween prize.

After she sniffed you, Mariana said you smelled nice.

Worth it.

So, yeah. You like smelling good for the girls. You like smelling like a man instead of a boy. Like sandalwood and lemon myrtle instead of Dove soap bars and strawberry-scented shampoo and baby powder.

Brody keeps eyeing the girls. He makes a show of scratching the back of his neck, flexing his bicep while acting like he's not looking their way. But they're not watching him at all.

He mutters an ugly word under his breath as he lets his arm fall.

You don't call him on it, though. He doesn't mean it. He's just joking around. And it's not like anyone but you hears him.

You, on the other hand, have basically sworn off cussing ever since *the incident*. You don't need an accidental repeat, so best not to get in the habit.

You pick the Camuto back up. "I'm gonna do this one." You've got Halloween money to spend on it. For some reason your parents always give you a card for Halloween, and some spending money, even though you don't know anyone else whose parents do that.

"Good, 'cause you stink." Brody throws his arm around your neck and gives you a shake and a quick "No homo."

You laugh and shove him away, but not too hard, because you're still in the middle of a Sephora and everything is stacked super precariously along the narrow aisles.

"Not as bad as you, my dude." You wave your hand in front of your face. "You sure you didn't fart back there?"

Brody's grin cracks open into a laugh so big it shows his molars. You don't often get a rise out of Brody, but when you do, you really do.

After, you and Brody pile into Marshall's car. You begged him to take you both to Sephora—your mom and dad were too busy with whatever they do on weekends—and you're still kind of surprised he agreed.

"Find what you needed?" Marshall asks as you buckle up. Brody's behind you, but he leans forward.

"He must've tried every single bottle in there twice," he says. "Even the sparkly pink ones."

You roll your eyes, but Marshall looks at Brody in the mirror. "What's wrong with sparkly pink things?"

Brody snaps his mouth shut and sits back. He's quiet the rest of the ride, though he gives you a quick fist bump as he gets out of the car.

On the way home, you say, "Did you have to come at him like that? He was just joking around."

"I know he's your friend," Marshall says. "But he doesn't get to talk like that. My car, my rules."

You cross your arms and bite your tongue.

Brody didn't mean anything by it.

You wish your brother wasn't so sensitive.

10

FARSHID

IN SEVENTH HOUR ON MONDAY, THE UNTHINKABLE HAPPENS.

You've moved on to a strength unit in conditioning, and your coaches have decided to use the buddy system to assign spotters.

And your buddy?

It's Dayton Reilly.

You've managed to avoid him ever since he shouted that word. Ignored him in history, evaded him in the halls, grabbed a warm-up spot as far away from him as possible in conditioning every day.

But now you're stuck with him on his knees, holding your ankles while you do your sit-ups.

Next to you, Angel Pacheco is doing the same for Brody Connors, and you're proud to find yourself outpacing Brody. Despite his gains (his arms have been looking impressive lately, solidly A-tier), it seems you've got the stronger core. You do thirty minutes of core every day at boxing, so at least it's paying off.

Dayton is counting your reps under his breath, though every so often he makes a funny face at Brody, which makes Brody laugh, and then Brody must do *something* because then Dayton laughs and shifts and smashes your toe with his knee.

"Sorry." He gets off your toe and draws his eyebrows together. "You're good at these."

You can't shrug while you're doing sit-ups, or nod for that matter, so you mutter a "thanks" between breaths.

"No homo," Brody huffs next to you, "but you gotta give me your ab routine."

No homo?

The exercise had driven it from your mind, but it all comes rushing back: who Dayton is, what he said, what he believes.

Who he hates.

Your rhythm slips for a second, you only do half a rep, and crap, you hate this feeling, when you mess up one and then your whole form falls apart.

You're stronger than this.

"Brody," Dayton says, but you don't know why. You're honestly surprised Dayton's even willing to spot you.

Not that he knows anything about you. Not that there's anything to know about you anyway. You don't think.

You might only be fourteen, but you're old enough to know that people who run around shouting what Dayton shouted usually shout other words, too. Words for people with brown skin, words for immigrants who come from places America looks down on even though America messed them up in the first place, words for people who are different in whatever way matters that day.

You've been holding your breath—you know better than to do that, but you were too distracted—so your core gives out on you and you collapse to the floor with a wheeze. You try to rise again but your abdomen gives a fluttering shake before failure, and you feel lightheaded for a second.

"Seventy-seven," Dayton says, patting your shins, but you

scooch out from under him as quick as you can. You don't want him touching you, don't want him judging you, don't want him saying anything for any reason whatsoever. You tug your shirt down where it's ridden up a bit. In addition to the hair on your upper lip, you've also started getting some around your belly button, dark coarse hairs that trail downward. You think about shaving them, too, except you kind of like that they give a little definition there, at least until you can get your body fat low enough to show some abs.

Dayton leans back and stands, offering you a hand, but you roll over and get up yourself. You feel a flash of fire along your rib cage before you hunch a bit, relieving the pressure from your screaming abdominal muscles.

"Farshid? You okay?" he asks.

"Fine," you say. Why is he asking, anyway? He doesn't care, couldn't possibly care. Maybe he was a Boy Scout, or maybe the sanctity of the buddy system matters more than all the bigotry, or maybe it's just the bro code, but you're *not* his bro and never will be.

Brody and Angel have finished, too. Brody shadowboxes Dayton for a second before giving a backhanded slap to Dayton's stomach. Dayton flinches away with a "Cut it out, man."

Brody just laughs and turns to shadowbox you instead. His form is atrocious, but his arms are really popping, straining the holes of his T-shirt. Did he order it a size too small? Maybe you should do that, too. Maybe that would make your own arms pop.

But form? There's nothing there. His feet are even, planted flat, and he's not rotating from his shoulder with his jabs, and there's no power in his cross because his fist isn't even crossing his body with his hips so square.

"Come on, square up," he says, bouncing back and forth, not even a proper bob, and then he throws another jab your way.

On the one hand, there's no way you're actually going to box Brody, there's no way you're going to box anyone, because while you like hitting the bag, the thought of hitting another person makes you want to throw up.

On the other hand, he's blocking you from the bench where you're supposed to be doing your presses, and even though you've gotten better at push-ups lately, your chest still needs work.

So you shift into a proper stance, weave around his fist the next time it comes your way, and—three-four-five—just miss him with a left hook, right hook, left uppercut. You don't touch him at all, but he almost trips and stumbles back until Dayton catches him, laughing.

"Let go," Brody says, shaking Dayton off.

Dayton does, but his blue eyes are full of mirth at the whole situation. He looks at you like he's impressed.

You shrug at him, smile a little. For a second you forget everything you know about him. He's just another guy in class, trying to make it through high school, laughing when his friend fooled around and found out.

But then you shift to Brody and your smile dies. His face is a storm cloud.

"You okay?" you ask, because you didn't mean to make him trip. And now you're hot all over, because you thought it was a game. But if it was, then why does it feel like you've lost?

"Whatever."

He turns, muttering under his breath as he goes to load the bar. His shoulders look broad and triangular and strong as he does it, and you wonder how he manages it, what lifts he does and how many reps, and what his macros are like, but you know you can't ask him about it now. You lost the chance as soon as you outboxed him.

You just don't know why.

11

DAYTON

FARSHID IS QUIET AS YOU HELP HIM RACK HIS WEIGHTS. HE GIVES you a terse nod and then heads to the locker room without you. While you were working out, you thought maybe he was thawing a little. You've spent the last two months sitting right behind him in history, being totally ignored every day. Not to mention run-ins in the hall, or after school. But he never talks. Never even looks at you. A couple of times you saw him turn around and go the other way when he saw you coming, and you're pretty sure he did it on purpose.

You could understand if he did it for, like, a week after *the incident*, but he keeps doing it. Like he's convinced you'll do it again. Like he thinks he knows everything about you based on one word. Six letters. A single mistake you've long since apologized for.

You thought being paired up with him might give you the chance to prove you're cool. And you thought maybe it was working for a moment, when he seemed to relax a bit. Actually speak to you. Give half a smile at Brody's antics. But then Brody went too far and got all huffy because he didn't know Farshid could box. Granted, you didn't, either. Who would've guessed? But Farshid was fast and sharp and controlled, and Brody got laughed at.

Brody hates getting laughed at.

His heavy brows are still drawn together as the two of you join the crowd headed to the locker room. The bell's going to ring soon.

"Good work today," you say, trying to lighten his mood.

"You too. Keep it up and you'll stop looking like a breadstick."

You snort out a laugh. "A breadstick? Cruel."

Brody cracks a momentary grin, but then he turns dour again. His eyes land on Farshid's back as he disappears into the locker room.

"Can you believe that little—"

And then he says that word.

"Brody!" You grab his arm. "You can't say that."

Brody shrugs you off. "Why? He can't hear."

It's true, Farshid can't. He's too far away.

But you can hear it. And you don't want to.

You never want to hear it again.

"You're the one who shouted it for the whole class to hear," Brody reminds you.

"Yeah, and I got in trouble for it. I don't want you to."

He just shrugs. "I've been in trouble before. I can handle it."

That's not the point. Brody's your friend. You don't *want* him to get in trouble.

And you don't want people to think he's a homophobe. You don't want people to think you are, either, but that ship's already sailed, and it sucks, because you're not.

You're *not*.

But some people still give you wary looks when they pass you in the hall. Last week Cora, this trans girl in the senior class, let a door close in your face after holding it for like five different people.

You want better than that for Brody. But you don't know how to say any of that.

So instead you say, "I'd be bored if you landed yourself in ISS again."

"Nah, I'd just get you in trouble with me so we could go together." Brody laughs, but then he softens. "I'd be bored without you, too, my dude. No homo."

"No homo," you softly agree.

YOU MIGHT BE CASSANDRA.

(You've been studying *The Iliad* in ELA. And every time Mr. Clemens talks about Patroclus and Achilles he looks right at you, like he's daring you to say something. Make some joke, some hateful comment. You're not sure if Patroclus or Achilles are really in love or if they're just best friends and ancient Greece was different. But either way, you're fine with it. If anything, Mr. Clemens should be paying more attention to Reggie, who *does* keep snickering. But Reggie never seems to get caught doing anything bad.)

(He still owes you twenty dollars, too.)

Anyway, you're not thinking of Patroclus and Achilles, you're thinking of Cassandra, who warned people about the future she saw and was totally ignored, because Brody is missing from conditioning on Tuesday. You and Angel and Farshid end up in a three-way spotting situation as you do squats and seated rows and planks.

"I heard Brody got ISS again," Angel says, leaning against the squat rack while you stand behind Farshid, ready to spot him if he needs it, but the dude is strong, stronger than you, with good form.

You're not sure what you could actually do if he did start to fail, other than fail with him.

You shake your head. "Really?"

"Yeah." Angel's a skinny guy—breadstick-shaped, like you—with brown skin, though his brown is a different, cooler brown than Farshid's. For such a breadstick-shaped guy, his voice is deep, like he's got a tuba in his chest. He's got a slight accent, a softening of the consonants that makes him nice to listen to. "Guess he made the jerking-off sign in bio after Mx. Lee called him out for goofing off during lab."

You groan.

Of course he did.

Of course he did.

In front of you, Farshid huffs, and you raise your hands in case he needs help, but he doesn't.

The guy's a freaking beast.

"I can't believe him sometimes," you say.

He's your best friend, but on days like this he's a total mystery, too.

Angel chuckles. "Tell me about it. For a guy who says 'no homo' every other sentence, he sure talks about masturbation a lot."

Farshid grunts, and this time you see his legs shake and the bar wobble. You get your hand under it in time, steady him, and then he finishes his set on his own. The back of his neck is getting dark, brown blooming to rust. You wonder if he's blushing because of nearly failing or because of what Angel said. Your own chest is tight with embarrassment. You're not even sure why, except that word still feels weird. Forbidden.

Exciting.

You still aren't sure how to do it. You'd look it up, but your parents have your phone on parental lockdown. Maybe if you hadn't gotten in trouble at the beginning of the year, they'd have loosened up, but no.

Your own neck and ears are warming, tingling, and you're relieved when Farshid finishes his set and racks the weight. He dips below it and straightens up, and yeah, he's blushing big-time. Just like you.

His eyes meet yours for a second. In the harsh lighting of the weight room, they look more amber than brown, with arched dark eyebrows above and thick lashes that brush his cheeks as he blinks. You hear the girls talking about him sometimes.

You wish they talked about *you* that way.

You give him a small, embarrassed smile, while Angel pulls off some of the weights Farshid added, because again: The guy's a beast.

Farshid smiles back for a second, and your stomach unwinds a bit because at least you're not the only one who feels weird about this whole conversation. But then it's like a door slams shut. The light goes out of his eyes, and a frown creases his lips.

He shakes his head and looks away, at the floor, at the walls, at anything but you.

And that looseness in your chest clenches up again, this time with a flare of anger.

"What's your problem with me, dude?" you blurt out.

Farshid looks back at you. "Problem?"

"You act like I'm . . ." You don't even know. He's just like your old friends. Like Cooper and Tyler. He acts like you're toxic. Like you're a walking hate crime.

"Why do you hate me?"

Farshid blinks at you. "Me? Hate you? You're the one who shouted a slur in front of the whole class. You're the one who hates people."

"I don't," you say. "It was a stupid joke. And I already paid for it."

"Paid for it? Three days of ISS. You never even apologized."

You realize people are pausing their workouts to watch you. Angel's staring, mouth dropped open, but you can't stop yourself.

"I *did*."

"Not to me."

"Well, I didn't know you were gay! I'm sorry!"

"I'm not!" Farshid shouts, and anyone who wasn't staring definitely is now. He's breathing hard, harder than he was when he was doing his squats. His head jerks around, taking in all the stares.

Then he's moving at you, and you think he's going to punch you. You think you might deserve it.

But he swerves around you, barely brushing past your shoulder, and stomps out of the weight room. The door shuts behind him with an echoing thud.

All the anger drains out of you. All the embarrassment, too. Instead, shame floods you. You're intimately familiar with the sensation by now. But this time is worse.

You *made* it worse.

You don't hate anyone.

Except maybe yourself a little bit.

12

FARSHID

THE BIRTH OF BAHÁ'U'LLÁH IS ONE OF THE MOST IMPORTANT HOLY days in the Bahá'í calendar. So important that you get to stay home from school, which is just fine, because after conditioning yesterday you never want to see Dayton or Angel or anyone ever again.

You can't believe you let Dayton get to you. What were you thinking, shouting like that? Insisting you're not gay is only going to make people think you are. And you're not.

You're not.

Cold anger creeps along your shoulders, down your arms, as you fill the giant water boiler in the Bahá'í Center's kitchen. Dayton acted like *you* were the one with the problem, when *he's* the bigot. He let the whole school know right at the beginning of the year. He showed everyone exactly who he was.

"When people show you who they are, believe them," Nadeem told you once, when you came home from fifth grade crying because one of your classmates—you don't even remember her name anymore—told you you were going to hell for not being Christian.

You weren't crying because you thought you were going to hell. You know you're not. You were crying because you thought you were friends, thought she accepted you as you were, but it turned out "accepted" really meant "pitying and praying for," and you didn't want that.

Madison. That was her name.

You haven't thought of her in a long time. You wonder what ever happened to her. She moved before middle school. Sometimes you're still a little sad how it all ended. You used to build LEGO sets together. She had this really sweet castle set with knights and dragons and wizards, which frequently got visited by your ninjas and the occasional Avenger.

You shake the thought away. There's still a lot of work to do.

"FARSHID, TAKE MORE THAN THAT," YOUR MOM TELLS YOU IN FARSI as you fill your plate.

You shake your head. You don't have your scale here to measure your portions, and you don't even know the macros on some of this stuff. Baba made khoresh bademjan, which is your favorite, but it doesn't have nearly enough protein in it. Khanum Varga made the rice, and she makes the best tahdig—even Maman grudgingly admits that—but you're avoiding white rice right now because it's way too many carbs.

It's not all Iranian food, though. There's lots of white Bahá'ís, too, and a few Black folks, and lots of immigrant families, not just Iranians. So you were able to fill your plate with some smoked chicken breast from a family who always brings really good barbecue to potlucks, and a big salad from a family doing the whole vegan thing, and some roasted asparagus from who knows where, but probably an Iranian judging by how overcooked they are.

You salivate over the beautiful golden macaroni and cheese someone brought, but that's definitely not on your plan. Your body fat is stubbornly hovering just above 10 percent, and if you could only get down to single digits, you know your abs would show, a four-pack at least if not the full six.

"I'm good, Maman," you say, sticking to English more out of annoyance than anything. You didn't go to the gym today—not on a holy day—and given the amount of food here, you really should've, but even Coach Nico says rest days are important. You just should've timed things out better.

"You barely eat anything anymore." She reaches for the rice paddle, scooping up a heap and catching a bit of the crispy tahdig with it, the golden brown wedge gleaming with oil, and tries to plop it onto your plate, but you swing it away.

"Nakon, Maman!" you say, that cold fire of anger rising up in you again. You don't even know why. You've lived your whole life with your mother showing her love with a full plate and an offer of seconds. You know she's genetically incapable of not feeding you. But suddenly you can't stand it: You don't want her carbs, you don't want her love; all you want is some space for once. "Can you just leave me alone?"

Your voice cracks as you say it, but still, it was loud, too loud for the Bahá'í Center. This isn't the gym back at school.

Your mother blinks and sets the rice back down.

"Farshid Nafari," she says, voice low. "Behave yourself."

"Then stop treating me like a little kid! Or a pig you're fattening up for . . . for . . ." What holiday do they eat pigs at, anyway? "My plate is already full! Would you stop nagging me?"

The room goes quiet as everyone looks your way. Shame wars

with anger inside you. Why does Maman have to make everything into a fight? Why does she keep trying to control you?

If you don't get away, you think you're going to explode.

You grab a fork and make your escape.

NADEEM FINDS YOU IN ONE OF THE CLASSROOMS AT THE BACK OF the center, eating in the dark. He snaps on the light.

You used to have Sunday school classes in here, not because Sundays mean much to Bahá'ís, but because that's the day most people have off because you all live in America, where they supposedly have separation of church and state, as long as you don't count Christmas being a federal holiday.

Everything felt so much simpler back in Sunday school, memorizing the months of the Bahá'í calendar, learning prayers set to music, making Ayyám-i-Há decorations out of construction paper.

Now the whole place feels like a weight, your mom dragging you here to clean the center on the weekends feels like punishment, your dad buried in emails from the Local Spiritual Assembly feels like abandonment.

You don't know what's wrong with you.

"You ever planning on coming out?"

Ice floods your veins, but Nadeem graduated from Meadowbrook last year and goes to KU now. He doesn't know what happened yesterday in conditioning. He doesn't know about his poor word choice.

Conversation and laughter flood in through the door, along with the soft sound of someone playing guitar. Sometimes it's hard to tell the difference between a Bahá'í celebration and a secular mehmooni. But there's not as much dancing at the former, you suppose, and way more white people.

When you don't answer, Nadeem flops into the seat next to you, but it's lower than he realized, built for ten-year-olds, and he nearly knocks the table over, so you have to steady it before your chicken goes flying.

"Careful," you say even though the danger's passed.

"I can't believe we used to sit at these." He looks around the room wistfully. Nadeem always liked Sunday school better than you, loved to show Maman and Baba how quickly he'd memorized the Obligatory Prayers or how he could still recite a dozen other prayers in Persian, English, and Arabic. You only know them in English.

"Thank God we don't have to anymore," you say.

"It wasn't so bad." Nadeem gives your shoulder a squeeze. "Whoa, is that muscle?"

You sit up a little straighter and try not to preen. Maybe your gains are finally showing a little bit after all. Maybe your shoulders have finally upgraded to B-tier.

"Maybe."

Nadeem releases you. "Baba said you were going to the gym every day. Are you getting your homework done?"

You sigh. "Yes, *Maman*."

Then it's Nadeem's turn to sigh. "You know she loves you, right? You're her baby. Sometimes you just have to put up with it."

You stare at Nadeem. After staying shaven all through high school, he's started growing out a neat beard. His square forehead is framed by his thick black hair, which he's cut into a stylish part.

You wonder if you'll ever look as confident as him. Right now you're just taller, and you've got a pimple right above your eyebrow, and your upper lip is a little red from where you either pressed the razor into your skin too hard or left it against your skin too long, you're still not sure which.

"Come on. Stop moping. You can mope at home." He tries to stand, has to grip the desk to get back up off the low chairs, and tries to pull you up. "When did you get so heavy?"

"Muscle weighs more," you say automatically, but you stand. You're half a head taller than him now, and that still feels weird to you. In memory he always towered over you.

In personality he still does.

He pats your arm. "Let's go. There's dessert."

You can't have any, but you follow your brother anyway.

13

DAYTON

SATURDAY, BRODY TEXTS AND ASKS IF YOU WANT TO HANG OUT.

Sure. Lemme see if my brother can drive me.

Bet.

You've only seen him after school the past three days, grabbing a few minutes to catch up before taking your separate buses. At least his parents don't ground him for making off-color jokes, even ones that land him in ISS, so you've been able to text, sharing memes and jokes and *my dude*s and even a bit of gossip.

Brody seems weirdly into gossip, wanting to know every little thing he missed. Probably because he feels isolated while he's in ISS. You get that: You felt alone while you were in it, too, especially that last day when you didn't even have Brody for company.

You also got to hear him—well, read him—complain about Ms. Anderson. He had creative names for her, some of which you already knew were swears, some of which you had to look up (also swears), and some of which are, as far as you can tell, Brody's own inventions.

But probably also said with the energy of a swear.

I'm just glad you're done. Conditioning sucks without you.

Haha yeah, getting stuck with a—

He types that word, what he called Farshid under his breath the other day. Well, the shortened version. But either way, seeing it spelled out is somehow worse.

Please don't call him that, you tell him. Plead, really, but he can't tell that from your text.

Lighten up man, just a joke.

You know from experience how a joke can get out of hand. But Brody's already had a tough week. You don't want to kick him when he's down.

Anyway meet at Zona? We can even go look at your fragrances.

Bet.

MARSHALL AGREES TO TAKE YOU.

But he has to pick up Jace along the way.

You used to get along with Jace really well. He used to let you watch him and Marshall play *Overwatch*. Even let you take a turn every now and then. He doesn't have any siblings, so he acted like you were his little brother, too.

Not anymore, though. Even though you've apologized—even though Marshall has actually asked him to lighten up a bit—he still treats you like a stranger. No, worse.

He treats you like a danger.

Even though you're pretty sure he could beat you up, if you truly were one. He's a little short for a basketball player, maybe, but he's still taller than you. His family is Korean, and he's got sleek black hair, and piercing brown eyes, and sharp cheekbones you've heard more than one girl in your class swoon over, despite him being unavailable. He's had a string of boyfriends all through high school, according to Marshall, including guys who aren't even out yet.

You wonder how many guys there are who aren't out yet. Do they think you're a danger, too? The thought makes your skin crawl.

You don't hate anyone. You don't *want* to hate anyone.

All because of that one word.

You can't believe Brody can throw it around so casually. But as long as he doesn't throw it around in front of Jace . . .

When you pull up at Jace's house, you offer to get in the back, but, like usual, Marshall stops you.

"You're my brother," he says. "Family gets shotgun."

That's always been Marshall's rule, even though you know he likes his friends better than you. It was even the rule when you were grounded and Marshall was mad at you.

"I don't mind," you mutter, but it's no use, because Jace knows the rule, doesn't even comment on it.

"Hey," he says, sliding in behind you and buckling up. His voice is clear and high and smooth, like a singer's. He should be in choir.

"Hey," Marshall agrees, looking both ways three times before backing out of Jace's driveway, even though there are no other cars in this little Gladstone cul-de-sac.

"Hey," you offer, but Jace ignores you.

You glance at your brother. His mouth tightens up a bit, like he might say something again. But then he doesn't.

He made it clear he loves you but he's not going to fix your messes for you. But you don't know what else to do. You took accountability. You said you were sorry.

Maybe some people are just never going to forgive you.

In the end, Marshall shakes his head and asks if Jace has done his trig homework.

You cross your arms and keep quiet.

BRODY'S WAITING FOR YOU OUTSIDE THE NOODLE SHOP, SO YOU wave at Marshall (and Jace, who ignores you again) and jog across the street even though the light is flashing red.

"Hey." You offer a hand, and he pulls you into a swift bro hug.

"Hey. You hungry?"

"Sure."

The mac and cheese is calling your name, so you get it topped with brisket and barbecue sauce, while Brody gets a huge protein bowl that's twice as big as yours. He holds his fork at an odd angle, and you clock him flexing his bicep as he twirls his noodles. It'd be impressive if it wasn't so obvious. But a few of the girls at the next table giggle, so maybe it's impressive enough.

You sit up straighter, in case they notice you, too. You're glad you did your hair before going out, though now you wish you hadn't rested your head against the car seat on the ride over. If your hair's messed up, it makes your skull look flat in the back. You comb your fingers through it to fluff it a bit.

At least you know you smell good. Even if you're still a breadstick.

"So, we going to Sephora after?"

You love that he asks, but you're actually good on fragrance for now. "Nah. What do you want to do?"

Brody shrugs. "We can check out the GameStop."

You're amazed he finishes off his entire bowl. You only made it through half your mac and cheese before you got too full. You hear your dad's voice in your head, telling you that wasting food is stupid, and your mom's voice, telling you to box it up and save it for later. But you don't want to carry mac and cheese around with you all day, so you end up tossing it.

The sun is out, and it's a little warmer today, warm enough you only need a light jacket. Brody's still in a T-shirt and shorts, though you could swear his arms are covered in goose bumps. And you're pretty sure you catch a shiver when he thinks you're not looking.

The sun feels nice as you follow the sidewalk past storefronts, take the turn into the center of the shopping district where all the fancier stores are, but also, crucially, the GameStop.

As you walk, Brody ribs you for messing up your audition for a solo in choir. You tease him for his abysmal performance in his latest *World of Warcraft* raid. You've never played it, but that doesn't matter. You're friends—best friends—and you know when to tease, when to give sympathy, and when to listen.

Brody listens as you tell him about the awkward car ride with Jace.

"Man, it's not like you've ever done anything to him," Brody says.

Which is technically true, depending on how you look at it. It wasn't like Jace was around for *the incident*.

"He's just being a drama queen."

"Yeah, but it still sucks. I don't know."

Brody scoffs. "Giving people the silent treatment is a major red flag."

You hadn't thought of it that way. But you suppose it is. You weren't as close to Jace as you were to Cooper or Tyler, but they all cut you out of their lives like you were never there to begin with.

You spend half an hour at GameStop, looking for deals on used games, taking a turn to try out the new ones on display when they're not being hogged by all the ten-year-olds whose parents don't let them have enough screen time at home. There's a cool vintage-looking Optimus Prime shirt on the racks, and unlike most of the stuff here, you can actually afford it. You surreptitiously check the size—yeah, it would fit—but you don't know if Brody used to like Transformers or if he would tease you for still kind of being into them.

Eventually, you get tired of the college-aged cashier at the checkout counter giving you the stink eye as you browse but don't buy, so you head back out.

"Hey, let's go to Barnes and Noble. I gotta pick up something."

"Okay." You didn't know Brody liked to read. Back when you were in ISS together, he acted like having to read after finishing his work for the day was a punishment worse than death. You kind of figured he hated books, but maybe he just hates the stuffy old books in ISS.

You read once that the smell of books makes some people have to poop. You're grateful you're not one of those people as you follow Brody toward the escalator to the second floor.

"What're you looking for?"

"The new *Star Wars* book dropped on Tuesday," he says. "I've been waiting all month for this."

You nod.

"What?" he asks.

"What what?"

You both hop off the escalator, in your case literally, because the little teeth at the top freak you out a bit.

"Why are you smiling like that?"

You didn't realize you were, but now that he's pointed it out, you smile wider.

"Didn't realize you were such a huge nerd."

He laughs and gives you a lighthearted shove toward the sci-fi section. You haven't spent much time in it. Truth be told, you usually go for the graphic novels a few aisles over.

Brody finds the one he wants—a chonker of a book, tall and wide and thick, with the edges sprayed black—and nabs it off the endcap. "They've got the special edition!" he says reverently.

His grin widens as he opens the book and flips through it, then goes back to the front and starts reading, standing there at the end of the aisle.

Like, really reading it. Not just staring at it. It's like he's tuned out the whole world.

You wonder how long you should give him. You've never seen him like this before. Brody's a bundle of energy, always moving. Now he's still, calm, and peaceful.

It makes you smile even wider.

You decide to leave him to his book, at least for a little while, and go check out the graphic novels, but when you turn into the aisle you stop short.

Tyler's at the other end.

You've known Tyler since fifth grade. You and Cooper used to go to his house after school to play UNO and watch movies and eat junk food.

But just like Cooper, he hasn't really talked to you since September.

Another guy judging you for one stupid mistake. A mistake that doesn't even affect him.

Anger rumbles in your stomach, warring with the smoked brisket from lunch. You want to shout at him for ditching you. You want to shove him into the bookshelves for being a terrible friend. For abandoning you instead of having your back.

Tyler used to be like a brother to you. But not anymore. Even when he was super mad at you, Marshall didn't abandon you the way Tyler and Cooper did.

Brody's a better friend to you than Tyler ever was. And you've only known him a few months.

You're about to turn and leave when Tyler looks your way. His mouth drops open in surprise.

He never did have much of a poker face, which made him super easy to beat in UNO. Super funny to frustrate, too, as he'd inevitably be the one made to draw twenty-four cards at some point in the game, all while he moaned and groaned and counted out his cards slowly.

"Oh," he says. "Hey, Dayton."

You're caught off guard. He actually spoke to you.

"Hey."

Tyler is tall and fat, his sweater stretching across his stomach. His red hair is cut short, and clear plastic glasses frame his hazel eyes. He's got a pimple coming in on his cheek, which makes you self-consciously reach for your own, where you've got one of your mom's pimple patches. You're not 100 percent sure they actually work, but Marshall swears by them.

"Long time no see," he says.

You expect him to brush you off, the way Cooper always does. Or ignore you, the way Jace did in the car. You don't know how to handle him acting . . . well, kind of normal.

But he doesn't get to act normal. That anger in your stomach blazes hotter, tempered with something cold it takes you a moment to identify.

You miss him.

You miss him, but you're also mad at him. Really, really mad.

How can he just stand there, acting like nothing happened? Like he didn't totally ditch you?

"Funny how that happens when you throw away four years of friendship," you say, surprised by how even you're able to keep your voice.

Tyler flinches, his cheeks flushing. Like you, he's super obvious when he gets embarrassed. Unlike you, he doesn't try to hide it. He just lets his face get red, looking at you with his eyes all magnified by his glasses like an anime character.

"There you are," Brody says from behind you. "You ready to go?"

Tyler looks from you to Brody and back. Like he's confused or something.

Just because he ditched you doesn't mean you don't have any friends.

"Oink, oink," Brody says, and Tyler's face goes even redder.

He gives you one last look, shakes his head, and retreats down the other end of the aisle.

You turn to Brody, who's back to smiling like nothing happened.

"Not cool," you say. You know Ty's self-conscious about his weight. Honestly, who isn't? It wasn't so bad in middle school, but since the start of this year, it's like everyone's obsessed with how they look in the mirror. Even you.

"What?" Brody asks. "Wasn't he one of the guys that acted like you were some kind of leper just because you got suspended?"

He was.

"You deserve better friends than that," Brody says, and the fire in your stomach banks, replaced with gentle warmth. Brody's not always perfect. Sometimes he says stuff he probably shouldn't—stuff you wouldn't—but he doesn't mean anything by it. And when it really matters, he has your back.

"Yeah," you say. "I do."

14

Farshid

"ONE, FOUR, FIVE," COACH NICO CALLS OUT.

Jab, right hook, left uppercut.

"Three, three, six." Left hook, left hook, right uppercut.

"One, two, one, two."

Jab, cross, jab, cross.

Sweat drips down your forehead into the corner of your eye, and you blink the salt burn away as you breathe and follow the combos. This is the best part of the workout, when you turn your brain off and punch as hard as you can, light on your feet one moment, driving from your hips the next. Butterfly. Bee.

You are strong and capable. You're getting gains.

You're not . . . that word.

You're not.

Coach Nico keeps calling out combos, but he grabs the back of your bag to hold it in place, staring right at you as you hit, nodding encouragement. Coach Nico is nothing like your coaches at school. He's young, for one, in his twenties, and used to do MMA, and now he works some sort of office job when he's not coaching thirty-something white ladies (and you) in a boxing class at five thirty in the morning. And maybe it's the fact that the class is like 80 percent women, but he's . . . kinder.

He still shouts out your combos in his sharp voice, he still corrects your form with a voice like a whip, but he does it because he knows you can do it, not because he thinks you can't, and he's always proud of you when you finally get it right.

He's tall, over six feet, with tanned white skin and buzzed black hair and sparkling blue eyes and a scar that bisects his right eyebrow that he probably got in the ring. But even though he *should* be kind of scary, when he smiles you can't help but smile back.

It's so different from the gym at school, where the guys act like every single thing is a competition that has to have winners and losers, except you're never quite sure what the win condition actually is.

Brody came back to class last week. He hasn't tried boxing you again, but he's taken to scowling at you every time you get too close, like a dog guarding a favorite chew toy.

You're still stuck with Dayton, but you don't really talk to him except about the workout, and he doesn't talk to you, either, and thankfully tomorrow's the last day of weight lifting so you can finally be free of him.

You don't picture his face on the bag as you hit it, but you do remember his voice screaming that word in the packed auditorium. Six letters. Six punches.

You pound the anger out of your chest, into the leather and sand.

"Time!" Coach Nico calls. A loud beep accompanies the end of the round, but you fire off your last combo one final time.

Coach Nico pats the bag as you step back. "Look at you go. You're like the Energizer Bunny."

"The what?"

He laughs at you and shakes his head. "Kids."

"I'm not a kid." You're fourteen.

"Then how come you don't know who the Energizer Bunny is?" he says. "All right, everybody, laps!"

You join the rest of the class, running laps around the edge of the ring, pushing yourself to go faster, savoring the burn in your legs, your shoulders, your lungs.

Faster, faster, faster, until you're flying, until you're outrunning everyone.

Everyone and every*thing*.

YOU NEVER KNEW COMMUNITY SERVICE WAS SO MUCH WORK.

"Ah, crap," Nour mutters as she tugs her keffiyeh out from where its tassels got smooshed between two boxes.

You and Nour and Cooper have been packing bunches of nonperishable foods to donate to shelters all across Kansas City. You've been at it for over an hour, and you're sweating in your shirt. It's seventy degrees outside—another wild fall day in Missouri—but the school's already turned on the heat after the temperature plunged below freezing last week, and once the heat's on, it stays on until spring, when the air conditioner gets turned back on.

"You good?" Cooper asks. He has a calm, soothing voice. He speaks softly, but you can hear everything he says. You wonder what he sounds like when he sings. You know he's a good violin player: He's third-chair second violin. You're third-chair cello yourself, but that's not nearly as impressive given there are only six cellos to begin with.

Sometimes you nod at each other as you play. Between orchestra and RC you might actually be approaching a solid B-tier friendship, but you're not sure. It's not the same as hanging out with Nour, where you can talk about anything and nothing and just come away happy and laughing. Everything with Cooper feels complicated, and you don't even know why.

You pull up your collar to wipe away the sweat beading your upper lip. You shaved again this morning, and it's sensitive.

"I'm good."

Cooper nods and passes you another box to tape shut. He's sweating, too, but while you can feel your deodorant starting to fail and have started keeping your elbows at your sides to trap any sweat in your armpits, Cooper smells . . . nice.

You can't help breathing in, flaring your nostrils, whenever he gets close enough to pass you another box of peanut butter and green beans and instant rice.

He smells like Maman's baking, sugar and almonds and fresh-ground cardamom, vanilla and toast and something else you can't identify.

"You smell good," you blurt out.

You wish you could take it back, grasp the words as they fly from your mouth and stuff them back in, knock them out of the sky, but your jabs aren't *that* fast.

Guys don't compliment each other on how they smell.

"No—" you begin to say, but Cooper's face breaks into the brightest smile you've ever seen.

"Thanks, man," he says. "It's my fall fragrance. It's not cloying, is it?"

You don't even know what *cloying* means, but if it's something bad, then no, it's not cloying. If more people smelled as nice as Cooper, maybe the world would have less problems.

The packing tape screeches across the top of the box as you secure it. When you turn to pass it to Nour to stack, she's staring at you.

"What?"

"Nothing." She shakes her head and takes the box.

"Seriously, what?" Oh God, can she smell you? You clamp your arms down again.

You put on extra deodorant after conditioning, but that just means your sweaty stink is mixed with *sea breeze*, whatever that is.

"Don't worry about it," she says. "Just thinking."

Your face is already flushed with exertion, so at least she can't see you blush from embarrassment. Neither can Cooper, who catches your eye and gives another smile.

All told, you and the rest of RC pack 212 boxes—enough to fill the big white creep van that pulls up to the main doors.

You and Cooper end up in the back of the van, stacking the boxes, and in here his smell is concentrated, even sweeter, and he's breathing hard, and as he hoists another stack of boxes his shirt gets caught and rides up, exposing his smooth brown stomach. It's soft, and tight, with a few wisps of black hair, and he smells nice, and *God no*, you feel that pressure in your boxers, that weird hook behind your waist, that fluttering in your chest.

You keep your back turned to him, think about your algebra homework, think about the cello part in Smetana's *Má Vlast* that you need to rehearse when you get home, think about the scorpion burpees Coach Nico had you doing this morning and what he might have in store for you tonight. You tug your shirt down over your waistband, wishing you had never decided to go down a size to show off your gains, and hope the creep van is dark enough to hide your awkwardness.

It's just the exertion, and the fact that Jina was banging on the bathroom door this morning so you had to make your shower super quick, and Baba told you about *hormones* and how it's normal to feel weird feelings, so honestly, you don't have to worry about anything.

It's not because of how Cooper smells, obviously.

"You good?" he asks again.

"Yeah." You push your sweaty hair off your forehead, then remember you're trying to keep your arms down in case you smell. "How many more?"

YOU'VE BEEN GOOD ALL MONTH. YOU'VE STUCK TO YOUR FOOD plan, hit your macros, said no to desserts and yes to vegetables and lean protein and brown rice instead of white.

But today, when Cooper says, "Let's see if there are any cookies left," you follow him and think you might actually eat one, because you love love *love* peanut butter cookies, especially if they've got that flaky salt on top.

Nour walks beside you, and she still looks put together, even though she worked just as hard as you. Her winged eyeliner is still in place, and her lipstick is still immaculate. The only sign she's been working hard is a small black smudge on the hem of her sweatshirt that she's trying to rub out with her thumb.

"You doing anything fun for Thanksgiving?" Cooper asks you.

"Not really."

Tomorrow is Thanksgiving, but it's also the Day of the Covenant, which means another big celebration and potluck at the Bahá'í Center.

You don't tell Cooper about the Day of the Covenant, though. You're not even sure why. It's not like you're ashamed or embarrassed, being Bahá'í. Your parents brought you across an entire ocean so you could worship freely, but somehow "freedom of religion" never seems to *quite* apply to you, not when everyone gets Christmas off but you have to take an excused absence for nearly every holy day that you actually celebrate.

"Just eating a lot," you finally tell Cooper.

Actually, now that you think of it, you'd better skip the cookie after all. Maman is sure to guilt you into eating off-plan, which is bad enough on its own, but the gym will be closed, too. You've been saving up your allowance, but you can't afford the weight set you want yet, and even if you could, Baba still doesn't want you to put it in the garage because he's worried about the dumbbells falling over and damaging one of the cars.

You don't think two days off is enough to sabotage your gains, but two days off combined with a bunch of starches and sugars? That's going to be tough. And even on Saturday, when the gym opens up again, Coach Nico will be off, and none of the other coaches are as good.

"What about you?" you ask Cooper.

He shrugs. "Checking out the Black Friday sales probably. My mom loves them."

"Sounds dangerous."

He laughs. "Yeah, for the other shoppers."

He's got a little gap between his top front teeth, and they're not as big as most people's, which makes his face very interesting as he laughs, makes you laugh along, too.

"What about you, Nour?" he asks.

You shake yourself, weirdly surprised that she's walking right beside you, because she has been the whole time, you were just talking to her, but somehow you had forgotten while Cooper was talking to you, and what is that about?

Maybe you need that cookie after all, need a bit of food to get your brain back on track until you can get home and drink your protein shake.

"We're all going to my grandma's in St. Louis."

"Oh, do you stuff your turkey with toasted raviolis and ooey-gooey butter cake?" Cooper asks.

You snort another laugh, and Nour gives you a look that could cut if she wasn't so obviously trying to suppress a laugh herself.

"As a matter of fact—" she begins as you round the corner back to RC's meeting room, but then she stops.

Cooper stops, too, and you almost bump into him. You look past his shoulder into the room, where other RC members are already staring at the whiteboard.

Someone came in while you were all out working.

Someone grabbed one of the dry-erase markers.

Someone wrote something on the board.

One word. Six letters. Well, seven this time, to make it plural.

You want to run and hide. You want to hit something.

You can't get away from that word, can't get away from the hate in people's hearts. Not hate for you, because you're not that, you're not one of those, but hate for your friends in here, your friends who spent all afternoon packing up food for hungry people, for children without homes, for grown-ups fleeing from bad situations, for people trying to start over because life dealt them a never-ending combo right to the heart and the soul and the wallet.

One word.

There's no escaping it.

PART 3

january

15

DAYTON

NEW YEAR. NEW SEMESTER. NEW YOU.

That's what's running through your mind as Marshall pulls into the student parking lot.

Everything is going to be better now.

Granted, the end of last semester isn't hard to beat.

Everyone thought you wrote that word on the RC board before Thanksgiving break.

You didn't. Obviously. You and Brody were long gone from school. You were at his house, and he was making you binge a bunch of old *Star Wars* cartoons you didn't even know existed.

That didn't stop the rumors flying when you got back from break. Or Dr. Matthews interrogating you in his office until he got hold of Brody's mom, who confirmed your alibi.

You're not proud of it, but your first thought was that Reggie had done it. You don't know why. But you didn't tell anyone. You weren't going to go throwing around accusations.

You're not that kind of guy.

And you're not the kind of guy who writes slurs on whiteboards, either.

You're not.

As you hoist your backpack, you spot Brody waiting for you by the doors and give him a wave. He's actually wearing pants today. Probably because the wind chill is below zero.

And he's wearing the ugly sweater you got him for Christmas.

In years past, you and the boys used to have a big Christmas bash, stay up too late, eat too many cookies, and exchange presents you saved your allowances up for.

There was no Christmas with the boys this year, but there was Christmas with Brody, which was nearly as good.

"Is Brody wearing that sweater you bought?" Marshall asks.

You crack a grin. It was calling your name at the store. Well, Brody's name. Brody laughed when he opened it, pulled it on right away.

"It's hideous, right?"

Marshall nods, but bites his lip.

"What?"

He shakes his head. "I just liked your old friends is all."

"Cooper and Tyler? The ones who ditched me?"

"That wasn't cool of them. But . . ." He gives a look toward Brody. "You know, Coach Strickland said we're all just combinations of the five people we hang out with the most. Is he really who you want to hang out with the most?"

"Brody's a good guy," you say. "He's my best friend. What's your problem?"

Marshall shrugs. "Forget it."

"He's a good guy," you say again as you trudge through the slushy parking lot.

Your brother only sees Brody's mischief. The times he goes too far, jokes too hard, gets ISS. He doesn't see Brody's kind side.

The side that patiently waits while you pick fragrances. The side that geeks out over *Star Wars* novels. The side that always has your back.

Brody's a good guy.

If Brody's not, then you're not, either.

"WER IST GUT IN DEUTSCH?" FRAU ASKS AS YOU GET READY FOR A quiz. You're one of the few people to raise your hands. Being *gut in Deutsch* is this thing Frau does where you basically bet on yourself that you can get 100 percent on the quiz, and if you do, you get bonus points, or *Pluspunkte*. But if you don't, you lose a letter grade on the quiz. You're not sure if that counts as gambling, or if it's her way of challenging you to build confidence in your German skills. But whatever it is, it's working. German's the only class you have an A-plus in.

You're not so stupid in German at least.

"The refrigerator." Frau's warm, round voice sounds almost foreign in English instead of German.

"Der Kühlschrank," you translate with a smile. *The cold cabinet*. So many German words are just two other words smooshed together into alarmingly literal descriptions. Like *Krankenwagen*, or *sick wagon*, which is the German word for *ambulance*.

Next to you, Mariana is smiling, too, the soft curves of her smooth lips curling up just a bit, revealing half a dimple. She got a new haircut over break. Her dark brown hair is still long, but it's only down to her shoulders instead of her back, and it's got a curl to it now. Or maybe waves. At this point you don't know the difference, because some girls get upset if you call their waves curls, and some girls get upset if you call their curls waves.

Curly or wavy, it still suits her. She looks nice, really nice, and whenever you see her you get this feeling like you drank too much Sprite and can't quite burp. It's hard to breathe, and your stomach feels like it might fly out of your body, leaving a hole in your shirt.

Mariana looks up at Frau but catches you looking at her, and her lips curl up a tiny bit more, deepening her dimple.

Your whole face goes hot, and you look away, focusing on Frau as she continues down this week's vocabulary list. It's all kitchen items. Stove, oven, microwave, table, chairs, plates, cups.

When it's done, you trade with Mariana to grade each other's quizzes as Frau goes down the answers, and your hand brushes hers. She has really soft hands.

She smiles at you again before turning back to grade your quiz.

You hope she notices you were *gut in Deutsch*.

You really do.

YOU'RE THROWN FOR A LOOP WHEN YOU WALK INTO CONDITIONING seventh hour and see Cooper.

You've barely spoken to him in months. Your moms still sent each other Christmas cards, though. You're not sure if it was habit or if they hadn't noticed you weren't friends anymore.

Surely they noticed you didn't have your usual Christmas party.

You manage to meet his eyes, and he gives you a little nod. But then he spots Farshid coming in behind you and actually gives him a wave and a smile.

Farshid waves back but then notices you looking and scowls.

Despite it being cold enough that even Brody wore long pants, Farshid's still in a tight T-shirt and shorts that show off his muscles. You wonder if he at least wore a coat or something, even if it's in his locker now.

He brushes past you but doesn't get that far since the two of you are stuck in the same row in the locker room.

You can feel his dislike rolling off him in waves, even with his back to you as he pulls off his shirt. You can't tell if his back has gotten bigger over break or if you're still just kind of freaked out by how muscular he is for a freshman, even more than Brody. He looks like some of the seniors on the wrestling team.

Should you be lifting weights more? Maybe more girls would notice you that way. But then again, you haven't heard about Farshid having a girlfriend, either, so who knows. You got some new fragrance for Christmas—a sampler pack from this Italian brand you read about on Reddit but can't actually get at Sephoras here—and a girl complimented you on the bus this morning, a junior, but then she went back to talking to her friends and acting like you didn't exist.

Girls are confusing.

Then again, it's not like guys are any better. Brody's your best friend, and you don't know what's going through his head half the time. And Farshid's quiet and angry for no reason as far as you can tell.

Sometimes, your dad likes to tease you and Marshall about being *hormonal teenagers*. You don't think you're that hormonal, but maybe everyone else is.

You're broken up into teams to start a basketball unit. You're not a fan of basketball, but it beats bowling, which you had to do once a week in eighth grade. You got bused to a bowling alley every Friday and then back before the bell rang, which meant you barely had time to bowl a full game.

As the whole class counts off into six teams, you luck out, because both you and Brody end up being fives. But so does Cooper, and you're not sure whether or not that's the worst possible luck.

Cooper is standing next to Farshid. He pats Farshid on the shoulder, while Farshid shrugs and scratches the back of his head. You watch his eyes following Cooper as he crosses the gym toward you and Brody, shoes squeaking.

You didn't know the two of them were friendly. Or friends? When did that happen, anyway? When did all your old friends find new ones?

Does Cooper talk fragrance with Farshid? Share memes? Have inside jokes? Your stomach twists. Even though Cooper and Tyler ditched you, you can't help missing them. A little bit. Sometimes.

Cooper was terrible at basketball in middle school, and you're relieved to see that hasn't changed, because you still suck, too. Brody's pretty decent, thankfully, and even though you're supposed to be doing three-on-threes to warm up, it's really just Brody-on-three.

Still, you "hustle" when your coach shouts at you, the only command you really understand, because you thought you already were on "defense." Andy, one of the guys on the other team, seems to have grown like six inches over break, so he's got reach on you.

Finally the whistle blows for teams to switch up. You breathe hard as you follow Brody and Cooper across the gym; Cooper reaches out and fist-bumps Farshid as you pass.

"I didn't know you and Farshid were friends," you say before you can stop yourself.

You're just curious, that's all.

Cooper shrugs. "Yeah. We're in orchestra together. And RC."

"When did you join RC?"

You don't know why you keep talking. Except this is the first time in forever that Cooper hasn't run away from a conversation with you.

"Back in September, after . . . you know."

After *the incident*.

You wonder if Cooper's queer and never told you. Or if he just wants to be an ally. Or if it's all just so people would know he was different than you. Like how he dropped you as a friend.

That anger that's never far starts simmering in your stomach. You're about to call him on it when Brody pipes up.

"Isn't RC the club for all the gays?"

Cooper bristles. You want to groan. You love the guy, but sometimes Brody can really stick his foot in his mouth.

"Rainbow Coalition is for everyone," Cooper says. "I'm an ally. Lots of us are."

Brody purses his lips. "Okay, but I bet it's a good place to pick up girls, right? You can do the whole *sensitive* thing they like. No homo."

"No homo?" Cooper raises an eyebrow. "What are you, twelve?"

"Just making it clear," Brody says. "Don't want any gays falling in love with me."

"I don't think that'll be a problem for *anyone*."

"What's that supposed to mean?"

You feel like you're watching a tennis match. Brody's taking the joke way too far. Normally you'd try to stop him, but seeing Cooper all flustered makes you want to laugh. A little bit.

Then Brody puffs out his chest and steps toward Cooper. Maybe it's gone too far.

"Guys," you warn, but Brody keeps going.

"Hey, I asked you a question. What's that supposed to mean?" He takes a step toward Cooper, but Cooper stands his ground.

"It means *no one*, gay or straight or anything in between, is going to fall in love with a guy who smells weird and jokes about jerking off all the time."

Brody's face twists, and you step closer, you're not sure why, but thankfully the whistle blows, sharp. You're supposed to be playing basketball.

Some team you make.

"Sorry," Brody tells you when you get another breather.

"What?"

"Sorry. I went too far," he admits. "That guy's such a faker, though. He acts like he cares about people, but all he really cares about is what people think of him. I remember how he ditched you last year."

You fight back a smile. Brody was just trying to protect you. The way friends do. The way Cooper and Tyler were supposed to but didn't.

You wish Marshall was in conditioning with you. So he could see this side of Brody. So he could understand.

"No worries, man." You give Brody a light punch on the shoulder. "Thanks."

16

FARSHID

"*PLEASE* TRY TO GET ALONG WITH YOUR MOM TONIGHT," BABA pleads, pausing at the door to the garage. "Please, Farshid-joon?"

It's not like you *try* to pick fights with her, but Baba doesn't understand.

Sometimes you're not sure you understand, either.

You nod and follow him to the car, letting Jina squeeze herself into the middle seat next to Nadeem before you get in after. You used to get stuck in the middle, being the youngest, but your shoulders are too broad for that now. You're finally seeing some real gains in them, getting that triangle shape you've been working on for months, but it's agonizingly slow going. Your body fat is still at 10 percent, though some mornings, if you haven't had any water yet and the light hits you just right, you think you might, *might*, be able to make out a bit of abs.

All that could go down the drain tonight, though, because Maman wants Italian for her birthday.

You clutch her card and her gift. You've been shoveling all the neighbors' driveways to make extra money. You're only a month into winter and there's been three heavy snows, which probably bodes poorly for the environment but boded well for your wallet, and for keeping you active when the gym was closed due to weather. Best of all, you were able to get Maman the silver bracelet Baba said she'd been eyeing. And you've nearly got enough for that weight set, too.

Bahá'ís don't really celebrate Christmas, so you didn't get any presents or money for that. You did get a new coat, though that was more because your newly B-tier shoulders didn't fit in your old one.

You've outgrown your dress shirt, too, which you only found out tonight when you tried to put it on. It's not just because of your gains (though that did feel good, no lie), but because you've gotten a little taller, too. You're wearing a polo shirt instead, one that was a little too big for you in the fall but now fits right, so you're a little underdressed compared to your family, but at least it's got a collar.

You keep quiet as Nadeem tells Maman and Baba about his first week back at KU—you're lucky the weather cleared enough for him to drive back for Maman's birthday. You stare out the window as you drive across the Missouri River and past CPKC Stadium, beneath those weird pylons and past the silver humps of the Kauffman Center, which look kind of like butt cheeks from a certain angle. Whoever designed it must've been good about not missing leg day.

"Farshid-jan?" Maman asks.

"Huh?" You weren't listening.

"How was your day?"

"It was fine," you say. You signed up to challenge for second chair at the end of the week, and you've been practicing hard, so you think you've got a shot at it. All your classes were fine. Even conditioning—which usually kind of sucks, having to share it with homophobes like Dayton and Brody—was a little better, since Cooper's schedule changed and he got moved to your class.

You hoped you'd be teamed up with him for the horrible basketball unit, but no, he ended up with Dayton and Brody. You're not sure which of them is worse.

You're not sure which of them wrote that word on RC's whiteboard, either. Maybe they did it together. Or maybe neither of them did. You've heard plenty of other people use that word.

No one got in trouble, though. There were no witnesses, no proof. Instead there was an all-school assembly about diversity and inclusion and fighting homophobia and you had to sit there, feeling weird the whole time, like everyone was staring at you, like everyone thought you were in RC because you're gay and not because you're an ally, because they know you like to look at Cooper sometimes, because maybe they're right, maybe that word *is* you.

One word, six letters. But if it's true, then nothing will ever be the same, will it?

You don't want it to be.

You don't.

YOU BREATHE A SIGH OF RELIEF WHEN YOU STEP INTO LIDIA'S, because you're not the only one here in a polo shirt instead of a dress shirt or suit, like Baba. In fact, there are people here in T-shirts and jeans, so you're actually dressed kind of nice in comparison.

Everything smells good: garlic and basil and tomatoes and burnt cheese and pasta water and lemon and coffee. You love Italian food. *Love* it.

It's the only other S-tier food, Persian being the first one of course.

Your mouth waters, and your stomach growls. You modified your afternoon snack, had a protein shake for lunch, just to make sure you wouldn't throw off your macros in this palace of carbohydrates.

The host shows your family to a table in the corner near a huge gas fireplace shielded from the rest of the room by thick glass. The whole restaurant is a converted freight house, with high ceilings and exposed wood beams. As you pull out Maman's seat for her, you catch a train whistle as it steams into Union Station to the south.

"Merci, Farshid-joon," she says as you scooch her back in and take the seat between her and Jina.

"Tavalodet mobarak, Maman."

You keep quiet, studying the menu as Nadeem talks about his new classes and Jina tells your parents about her plans for the Sweetheart Dance next month, which boy she's going to ask, where she wants to go for dinner, and what color dress she wants.

You don't have any stories to share about school, though. You didn't tell your parents about that word on the whiteboard back in November, and you didn't tell them about the assembly when you got back from Thanksgiving break, and you didn't tell them about how there's three more teachers at Rainbow Coalition meetings these days. They say they wanted to sign up as cosponsors, but they stand around with their arms crossed, and you get the feeling they're really just guards.

Four times a year—sometimes more—you practice what to do if someone brings a gun to school. You know how to barricade the doors, you know what to do if you get stuck in the hall or, worse, a bathroom, you know to silence your phone, you know what you'd do if . . .

But you've never practiced what to do if someone brings a hateful word to school.

Maybe there's nothing you can do.

Jina elbows your side. You didn't even notice the server come over. A college guy, you think, with a stylish amount of scruff on his cheeks and chin and upper lip, and gorgeous brown hair, and his shiny brown eyes stare at you, waiting. You hope the light in here hides the blush creeping up your neck and cheeks.

"Oh. Uh. Just water."

"And your meal?"

You swallow. The guy's slender but toned, and you wonder how much he eats per day, how much time he spends at the gym, what he does to look like that. He probably doesn't feed his face with the endless pasta trio.

"The house salad? With chicken?"

"Anything else?"

You shake your head.

"I'll have everything right out. Ah, and here's your bread." Another server comes up with a basket full of bread and several spreads. The bread smells heavenly. It's golden brown, gleaming with oil.

You definitely have to avoid it.

"Don't you want bread, maman?" your mom asks in Farsi.

"No, thank you," you answer in English. Birthday or no, you can't sacrifice your gains. Not when you're so close to your goal. You've got your macros figured out. Protein and vegetables. That's the plan.

But Maman frowns at you.

It's her birthday.

"I'll take a taste." You can always run an extra mile tomorrow.

YOU'RE SITTING ON THE FLOOR, YOUR CARD BOXES SCATTERED around you, working on a new Magic: The Gathering deck when Maman knocks on your door. You know it's her because she always knocks softly. Baba gives a sharp rap, and Jina gives two short taps, and Nadeem is a jerkwad who jiggles the handle and then opens it whether you say come in or not.

Sometimes you worry he'll walk in on you at exactly the wrong time, but then again, maybe that would traumatize him so much he'd stop. It'd traumatize you too, though, so you're grateful he's only here for the night before driving back to Lawrence for his morning class.

"Baleh?" you say, and your mom steps in. She's changed out of her dinner clothes and into pajamas, but her hair and makeup are still done, and her gold earrings still dangle to tickle her cheeks. The new bracelet you got her shimmers on her right wrist. It clashes with her other bracelets, which are gold, but she was ecstatic when she opened it, so she must not mind.

"Farshid-jan, can I talk to you for a minute?" she asks in English.

"Okay?"

She sits on your bed, toward the foot where it looks a little more made.

To be clear, it's *not* made, you just tossed your covers back on it before going for your run this morning, but it looks made because it happened to land that way.

Maman pats the bed next to her and you take a seat. She wraps a hand around you to squeeze your shoulder for a moment. "You're getting so strong."

You shrug. You've still got a ways to go, but you're getting there.

"You work hard."

You shrug again, looking at your hands. You've got calluses on the undersides of all your fingers from the weights. And on your knuckles, from the boxing.

"Thanks," you mutter.

You do work hard. Not hard enough, though.

Maman goes quiet. She rests a hand on your arm.

"You didn't eat much at dinner."

"I had plenty." You had the bread, and you had your salad, which was *huge*, and the grilled chicken it came with. You even tasted a bit of Maman's birthday tiramisu, which was probably more sugar than you've had the past month.

"I'm worried about you, joonam."

"Why?" Your chest gets this weird tightness. "I'm fine."

"Do you need to talk to someone?"

That flutter gets stronger, flapping against your rib cage.

"About what?"

God. Does she know?

How could she?

Did she see you looking at the waiter? You were just admiring his workout routine. And his hair, actually, you wonder if you could style your hair that way, but it was a totally normal thing.

"I'm fine," you say, louder than you mean to. "I don't need to talk to anyone."

"Farshid. It's not normal to work out so much. Twice a day—"

"Lots of teams do two-a-days," you say. "Football, swimming, soccer . . ."

"Do they starve themselves?"

"I'm not starving myself, Maman." You gesture to your frame. You can't build muscle if you don't eat enough. That's not how it works. "I eat twice as much as Jina. Or you."

It's just not a bunch of sugar and carbs. It's protein and fiber and vegetables and healthy fats, and it's not her business anyway. What does it matter to her? She doesn't know what it's like. She doesn't get it.

She never gets it.

"I'm just watching my macros," you say, and you're not sure where the venom in your voice comes from, but no, it's from how annoyed you are, because why is your mother constantly on your case? She's got two other kids to bother. "Would you stop nagging me?"

"I'm not nagging," she says, and her calmness annoys you, too. "You're fourteen, Farshid-jan; it's okay if you don't look like a bodybuilder. It's not healthy."

"No, eating every khoresh and every dessert and every single thing that crosses my path isn't healthy!" you shout. "Maybe you should worry about yourself instead of me!"

You hate yourself as soon as you say it. Your mother is beautiful.

You don't know what's wrong with you, but you can't stop. It's like there's a weight on you, smashing you into the carpet, pressing so hard you think your floor, your house, your whole neighborhood might collapse and fall into the center of the earth, and it's all you can do to fight against that inexorable pull.

"I know what I'm doing! I'm not a child anymore! I don't need you fattening me up like a pig! Can't you just leave me alone?"

Your mom looks like she wants to say something, and you wish she would. You wish she would yell back at you. You wish you could both shout and shout until you blow the roof off the house and the tempest inside you explodes into the stratosphere. But instead, her eyes sparkle. She blinks, too quickly, her mascaraed lashes fluttering like butterfly wings, and great, *great*, now you've made your mother cry, on her birthday no less.

You want to tell her you're sorry. You want to tell her you don't know why you're this way.

But you do know, don't you? You just don't want to admit it.

She gets up and closes your door behind you, and you feel like garbage, like dirt, like mud.

You wish you could go for a run, hit a heavy bag, do anything to exercise, exorcise, all this anger choking you, suffocating you, drowning you.

All this fear dragging you down.

You're afraid.

So afraid.

That weight presses on you again, like your bedroom is made of quicksand, and you wish it *would* drag you down, pull you out of this life and into another one far, far away, where you don't have to feel this way.

But all you can do is grab your pillow and cover your face and scream.

17

DAYTON

"SERIOUSLY, MY DUDE, DON'T YOU HAVE ENOUGH?" BRODY ASKS AS you sample the new Bvlgari. It's a bit spicier than you'd normally go for, but something about it is calling your name. It's warm and smooth and complex, perfect for winter. Perfect for Valentine's Day. Not that you have a Valentine. Or a date for the Sweetheart Dance.

It's not like you can ask someone. Girls ask the boys for Sweetheart; that's how it always goes. Though you wonder what happens if it's two girls. Or two boys. Or what happens if one or both are nonbinary? Who asks then?

Why does it have to be so complicated anyway? Can't you just get assigned random dance partners like you do for group projects? Or count off, like in conditioning?

You think about Mariana Herrera, who's been smiling at you every day in German, and wonder if she's asked anyone to Sweetheart, or if she even wants to go.

You don't think about her dimples.

Okay, maybe you do.

"Rebel Base to Dayton. Come in, Dayton," Brody says, talking into an imaginary headset.

You give him a playful shove. "First, you can never have enough fragrance, because you never know what kind of day you're going to have. What the weather will be like. What kind of mood you'll be in. It's good to have options. And second, I can't afford it anyway, but it's nice, isn't it?"

You waft the sampler in Brody's direction. His eyebrows rise up, like he's thinking about it, but then his eyes slide past you and he swats you away.

"Quit it man, you're being super sus right now."

You glance over your shoulder at the cluster of girls trying on fragrances of their own.

"I'm not being sus," you say. It's not gay to offer him a sample of cologne, especially on a slip of paper.

It's not like you made him sniff your collarbone, the way Mariana did that one time.

"Why are you smiling at me like that?" Brody asks. "I don't like you like that, man."

You roll your eyes. "I'm not smiling at you. I'm just smiling."

"Uh-huh. You're thinking about Mariana, aren't you?"

You try not to smile wider, but Brody can tell.

"You're in looooooove," Brody teases.

"Cut it out."

But his grin just widens. "I bet you lie in bed every night thinking about her while you whack it."

He makes the gesture again, though lately he's taken to doing it down between his knees, like that's how far he has to reach, which you're pretty certain is not only an exaggeration on his part but anatomically impossible as well.

You try not to react, but your face is heating up. Your stomach is clenching. Your smile is slipping. There's no way Brody could possibly know that you did it for the first time over break. No earthly way. It's not like there's a neon sign over your head or something.

But, well, yeah, you might be doing it most nights now. And yeah, maybe you think about kissing Mariana sometimes. You can't tell Brody that, though.

You can't tell him anything about it. Not how awesome it feels (and it *does* feel awesome). Or how weird you feel after (super weird). You're not sure if it's shame or guilt or just, like, hormones. And you're not sure if you *should* feel shame or guilt or hormones, either.

You wish Brody was the kind of guy you could talk about that stuff with. He's your best friend. But he jokes about it so often, you're afraid he won't take you seriously. Or worse, turn on you, the way your old friends did.

You can't risk it.

So you bottle up the shame and the guilt and the exhilaration and the thought of Mariana's dimples and you hold them tight.

Brody mimics fireworks exploding out of his hand, and you cringe as he cackles. "Come on, man, pick something. I'm hungry."

YOU WIND UP AT THE STARBUCKS INSIDE THE BARNES & NOBLE, YOU with a lemonade and Brody with an iced latte made with oat milk. You've known the guy for months now but somehow you've only just realized he's lactose intolerant. You never noticed him avoiding cheese at lunch, but now that you look back, he's never had the pizza. You thought he just didn't like it.

He's in the middle of telling you about the latest *Star Wars* novel he's reading when he sits up straighter, puffing his chest out a bit. He's in a black sweater today, and he pushes the sleeves up his forearms while looking past you.

"What?" you ask.

"Don't look," he says, then sticks his tongue out at you. "It's your girlfriend."

Your—

"Mariana?"

You're about to turn, but Brody kicks your shin under the table. "I said don't look!"

But looking couldn't be any more obvious than the "Ow!" you let out.

"Dayton?"

Now you *have* to look.

"Oh, hey!" you say. You swallow hard, then wonder if you look weird when you swallow. What are people supposed to look like when they swallow? But your mouth and throat feel dry. All that lemonade.

Mariana's in a light purple puffer coat that brings out the warm undertones of her sepia skin. Her eyebrows are two perfect arches over her rich, honey eyes. Her dimples deepen as she smiles at you over her coffee cup. It's a hot one, and you wonder what kind of drink she gets. And whether she adds flavors. And how many shots she likes. And whether she does whipped cream on top.

You wonder if she thinks you're basic for getting a lemonade, and you vow to develop a better palate for espresso so you can talk about coffee and lattes and breves and whatever else it is that Starbucks makes.

"Hey," you say again, scratching your chin and then yanking

your hand away, hoping she doesn't notice the remains of yesterday's pimple.

You can feel Brody's eyes on you, sense the glee he's barely containing, but you ignore him, because Mariana is looking at you. She's *smiling* at you.

You smile back.

"Um. Do you like coffee?"

Do.

You.

Like.

Coffee.

You want to face-palm. She's literally holding it right now.

"It's okay," she says. "Is that lemonade?"

You nod. "It's not as good as coffee, though."

"Oh. Cool."

Your heart feels like someone's stuck it on the milk foamer. You wonder if it would be easier to talk to her in German, but when you try to think of something to say, every word you know in German flies out your ears except *der Krankenwagen*.

"Are you going to Sweetheart?" you blurt out.

Mariana's smile softens. "Maybe. I haven't asked anyone yet."

"Oh."

You stifle a grunt as Brody kicks you under the table again.

"No one's asked me yet," you say.

Wow.

Subtle.

Why is this so hard?

"Oh my god," Brody blurts out. You spin back to face him. "Would you two get a room already?"

Mariana's smile falls. "Excuse me?" she says.

Your face isn't the only thing that's hot now. Your skin is on fire. Your chest, too.

"Brody—" you warn, but he keeps going.

"If you don't ask him to the dance, he might die of blue balls."

Mariana's face twists. She backs away, shaking her head.

"Wait," you say, trying to get up, but your ankle gets caught on the chair leg and you stagger as you stand, nearly upending your table.

"Whoa!" Brody says, trying to right it, while you step toward Mariana, but she keeps backing away.

If the eyes are the window to the soul, someone closed the blinds in hers.

"I'll see you around, Dayton."

She turns and goes.

You're not hot anymore, you're cold. You think you want to cry.

You don't cry. You're not going to. Definitely not in this Starbucks full of strangers.

Definitely not in front of Brody.

You turn back. Brody's mopped up the spilled latte and is trying to gather up the ice from your lemonade.

"You wanna help clean up your mess, man?"

You run to the counter and grab a wad of napkins, yanking them out of the metal holder thing when they get stuck, so some of them rip in the corner.

"How could you do that?" you ask as you scoop ice back into your plastic cup.

"Come on, it was just a joke."

"You were supposed to be my wingman."

"You know you have to try to land the plane at some point, right?"

"You totally grossed her out." You're whisper shouting, but even so, people are staring.

And Brody looks . . . hurt?

You're not sure. His shoulders are drawn in. He's rolled his sleeves back down. He's slouching.

"I was just trying to make her laugh. I didn't mean anything by it," he says softly. "I'm sorry, man. Really. I wasn't thinking."

"You always say that," you spit out before you can stop yourself.

And if Brody looked hurt before, he looks full-on sad now. Like *he* might be the one to cry.

All the anger from earlier dissipates.

You know what it's like to speak without thinking.

"Sorry," you say. "I just really like her."

"I know, man." Brody straightens up. "I'll make it up to you. Promise."

"Bet." You glance down at the table. His *Star Wars* novel took the brunt of the latte. "Sorry about your book."

"All good. I can get another one."

You're glad for that at least.

But how are you going to get another chance with Mariana?

18

FARSHID

"COME ON, ENERGIZER BUNNY," COACH NICO SAYS. "THREE MORE."

You breathe, engage your core, and lower the bar to your chest. Your arms are burning, your chest feels like it's being ripped in two, but you exhale and push the bar back up. Your left arm wobbles a bit, and Coach Nico almost grabs it, but you steady yourself.

"Eight," he says. "Two more. You can do it."

You can't. Sweat stains your shirt, runs down your temples to the black leather of the weight bench. You have a vision of dropping the bar onto yourself, crushing your windpipe, your body thrashing and going still as you suffocate.

You can't do two more.

You have to.

You grit your teeth and pump out another. "Nine. Last one, come on, Farshid."

Coach Nico says your name right. It took him months of practice, practice he insisted on doing, asking you over and over to say your name the way it's supposed to be said.

So, yeah, he can say it right, but still, he usually calls you Energizer Bunny.

You lower the bar, rest it on your chest, press back up, but you can't.

You can't.

You breathe deep and try again, but your arms have turned to spaghetti. There's nothing.

Coach Nico gets his hands under the bar to spot you.

"I'll help you. Last one. Together now."

You're not sure how much of the weight he's taking, but it's enough for you to get the bar off your chest. You press up with a grunt.

"Ten! Back down easy."

You try, arms wobbling, but then they give out. Thankfully Coach Nico catches it, taking all the weight and racking it. Your arms fall to your sides as you groan.

Coach Nico pats your chest, which feels like it's permanently cramped. You flinch.

He offers you a hand and helps you sit. You shake your head.

"I thought I had it," you manage between gasps.

You started out strong, your first two sets, but then everything fell apart on this one.

Coach Nico chuckles. "Don't be so hard on yourself. Think about where you started!"

When you started, you could barely press the bar by itself. Forty-five pounds.

Now you can do nearly three sets at a hundred and fifty.

"I guess."

Coach Nico furrows his brows at you. "Seriously, Farshid. You've come a long way. You should be proud of yourself. *I'm* proud of you."

You shrug and try not to let your smile show. You're glad he's proud of you, and you're proud of yourself, too, a little bit at least, but you're still not where you want to be. And you still don't look the way you need to.

The way you want to, you mean.

Coach Nico makes you stand and clasp your hands behind your back, helping you raise them to stretch your pecs out. You stifle a grunt of pain.

"When's the last time you took a day off?" he asks.

You try to remember. The gym was closed New Year's Day. And the day after. And then that snow day two weeks back.

"Couple weeks ago," you tell the floor. Yeah, that snow day, but what's the difference if it was one week ago or five? You feel fine. You don't need days off. You need to get stronger. Run faster. Punch harder.

"Rest is good for you." He releases your arms and you stand up. "You doing anything for Valentine's? I bet you break all the hearts at school."

You're still too sweaty for any blush to show, but you feel it starting anyway.

You shake your head.

Coach Nico laughs and goes over to the long bench with cubbies beneath it. He sits down, legs sprawling out, and motions for you to do the same.

You sit on the floor across from him instead, doing a pretzel stretch. But when you look up, he's staring at you, and he's not smiling. There's a little line between his eyebrows.

"I'm serious, Farshid. Rest days are important. So's eating right."

"I track my macros."

He sighs. "Right doesn't just mean macros. You're fourteen. You should be eating pizza and candy sometimes, too."

"I'm good." Pizza? Candy? No freaking way. That would throw everything off. All your hard work. All your careful planning.

"Just remember, the point of all this is to feel fit," he says. "As in capable of doing work. Not to look some kind of way in the mirror. Okay?"

"I know," you tell him. "I just want to be strong."

You just want to look right. For your shirts to fit your shoulders and show off your arms. For your shorts to sit at your waist, above your hips and glutes, just so.

"I still eat pizza." Or at least, you could if you wanted. "I'm good. Really."

You're not. Good, that is. But you don't know how to explain it to him. How doing this—working out, eating right, looking the way you need to look—is your best defense against what's out there. Against what people are saying about you, thinking about you.

Against that word.

"Okay. Good. I know I'm just a boxer, but you can talk to me, okay? Lots of guys get into their own heads about this sort of thing. I don't want that for you."

"Thanks." And you mean it. You're grateful Coach Nico has your back.

He looks past you at the clock on the wall. "Crap, we're out of time. Sorry to rush you, but I've got to head out. Got a suit fitting."

"Suit fitting?"

"Yeah. My sister and her girlfriend are finally getting married."

You didn't know Coach Nico had a sister.

You didn't know she was queer, either.

But your chest relaxes, as much as it can at least, when all the fibers of your muscles feel like they've superglued themselves to each other in a permanent clench.

You don't know how to tell him about yourself, though. Even thinking about it makes you feel like you've swallowed a dumbbell and it's lodged in your throat.

So you just say, "Cool."

IT'S HARD PRACTICING CELLO WHEN IT FEELS LIKE YOUR ARMS ARE going to fall out of their sockets, but you've got to if you want to keep second chair, or maybe even challenge for first.

You're still shaky, even after your post-workout shake. Dinner's not for another hour; the minty-sweet smell of Maman's khoresh karafs fills the house. You can't have rice with it, but the stew itself you can eat, since it's basically just beef and celery and herbs.

Two sharp taps on your door make you look up from your music. You're doing Holst's *The Planets*, the orchestra and the band all together, for the spring concert.

"Yeah?"

You set down your bow and push your hair off your forehead. It's getting kind of long, almost to your eyes, and Maman asked if you wanted to go for a haircut last weekend. You kind of did, but you'd been fighting with her that day about your chores and how it's not fair you got so many of Nadeem's old ones while Jina's are more or less the same, so you said no, because you didn't want to be stuck in a car with her, and she doesn't get to tell you how long to keep your hair anyway.

You hear Jina muttering outside your room, a few high-pitched giggles, but the door stays shut. You roll your eyes.

"Yeah?" you say louder.

This time the door swings open, revealing your sister and her two best friends, Audrey and Celeste. They're both juniors like Jina. Audrey's short and Desi, with rich brown skin and silky black hair and hazel eyes. Celeste's family is Chinese. She's taller and curvier, with her reddish-brown hair (dyed, you think) in a pixie cut. She wears sparkly eyeliner.

Much like you and Nour, Jina has found it easier to be friends with other immigrant kids. Or immigrants' kids' kids. Or whatever. You're not sure what generation they are, just that the three of them have been a unit since Jina was in eighth grade and you were in sixth and everyone asked if you were Jina's brother and she kept telling everyone *no* to protect her reputation.

From what, you never really found out.

Audrey giggles again and elbows Jina, who rolls her eyes but looks at you.

"Hey, Farshid. You going to the dance?"

You shake your head warily. No one's asked you, and you don't think you want to go anyway, because you're not sure you even like the idea of a dance. Why is Jina suddenly so invested anyway?

"How come?" she asks, cocking an eyebrow. It's perfectly shaped. She got her brows threaded last week, her and Maman both, even though Baba's the one with the hint of a unibrow.

"I dunno," you say. *No one asked me* would sound pathetic. *I don't want to* would sound suspicious.

You're trapped.

Jina looks to Celeste. They somehow manage to have an entire conversation consisting of eye contact, a few eyebrow lifts, and an occasional jerk of the head in your direction.

Finally, Audrey takes matters into her own hands, pushing Celeste forward so she stumbles into your room.

Celeste clears her throat. "You know my sister, Hope?"

You nod. She's in orchestra with you. She plays the viola, which is probably the best instrument after cello, though you'd never tell Cooper that.

Celeste waits, like you're supposed to say something.

"Yes," you say aloud, in case she didn't see your nod. You glance at Jina, who rolls her eyes and elbows Celeste again.

She sighs. "She thinks you're cute."

"Oh."

It's warm in your room with four people suddenly in it, but maybe that's not the only reason your cheeks are heating up. Your ears feel full, like you're on a plane about to land. You swallow.

On the one hand, you're glad someone thinks you're cute. Maybe she's noticed all your gains. Or maybe she likes your longer hair and the way it curls. Maybe you should keep it this length, even though it's annoying to have it always falling into your eyes.

On the other hand, you're pretty sure you don't care if girls think you're cute. You can't tell anyone that, though.

Jina and her friends wait in silence. Are you supposed to say something else?

"Th-thank you?"

Jina mutters, "Told you so."

What did she tell them? Your ears get hotter. What do they think about you?

Has Jina said anything to Maman and Baba?

"What?" you ask, though your throat has gone all sandy.

Jina throws up her hands. "I told you he was clueless." She turns back to you. "She wants to ask you to the dance, Farshid."

"Oh."

Well, why didn't she, then? Instead of going through messengers who can barely stop giggling long enough to ask the question.

"So . . . ," Audrey says.

"So?"

"So are you going to go?"

"I don't know," you say. "She hasn't asked me yet."

Jina snorts. "See? Oblivious. Come on. Tell Hope she's on her own."

Jina drags her friends out of your room, failing to close your door, so you rest your cello in its case and get up to close it.

Your hand shakes as you do, and this time it has nothing to do with exhaustion from your workout and everything to do with the surge of adrenaline racing through you.

A girl. Wants to ask you to the dance.

You could say yes. Everyone would see you together.

You wouldn't have to worry about that word, the whispers, the questions. Everyone would know you're straight.

Except you're not, are you? When you think about the dance, you don't think about Hope.

You think about Cooper.

So what should you do? Lie and go?

You don't know.

And you can't ask Jina what to do. You can't ask anyone in your family, because Maman and Baba might found out, and you can't ask Nour, because she already looks at you funny sometimes when you're in RC and Cooper is around, and you even heard her muttering something about "a man crush."

No one can know.

What are you supposed to do?

19
DAYTON

"HEY, COULD I BORROW SOME YSL?" MARSHALL ASKS, POKING HIS head into the bathroom you both share as you try to straighten your tie in the mirror.

Your dad was supposed to help you, but he ended up with a last-minute work emergency. He's been down in his office for over an hour. And your mom just said to ask your dad again when he was done. So you ended up searching for a video online.

Okay, three videos. Ties are complicated.

Marshall's own tie is still untied, and you wonder if he's in the same boat you are.

"Sure." You pass him the bottle. It's one of your favorite scents, but it's not really in your winter palette.

Marshall spritzes himself, then stands next to you at the mirror and starts working on his tie.

"You look good," he says.

"Thanks. You too."

Marshall's suit is a lighter gray than yours, with a bright green tie to match his date's dress.

"Whatever happened to that girl you liked? How come she didn't ask you?"

"Mariana," you say, then wince. You wish you could unsay it. It's too embarrassing.

"Yeah. What happened?"

You shrug.

"Come on. You said you thought she liked you back."

"Yeah, well." You don't want to get into it. Brody still feels bad about it.

He's the one who suggested you go stag together (though he insisted it was *no homo*). At least you won't be the only freshman without a date.

"Come on." Marshall elbows you in the side.

You bite your lip.

"We ran into her at Zona a while back."

"Ah." Marshall frowns in the mirror. "Something happen?"

You roll your eyes. "Brody made a joke that didn't land. You know how he is."

Your brother's eyes get stormier beneath his brows. "I know he's kind of gross to girls."

"He's not! He just has chronic foot-in-mouth disease." He already apologized. Besides, he promised to help you talk to Mariana and maybe even get a dance.

Marshall just shakes his head. "Whatever you say. You almost ready? I'm supposed to pick up Lex in half an hour."

Lex is the junior Marshall is going with, as "just friends," even though you think your brother might have a crush on her.

You tug on your tie. This might be as good as it's going to get.

"I'll be ready."

"MAN, HOW DID THAT FREAK PULL SUCH A HOTTIE?" BRODY mutters into his soda.

You follow his gaze out to the dance floor, where Farshid is slow dancing with Hope Wang, a cute girl you have choir with. They look like they're having fun.

You, on the other hand, are not. You've spent the whole time hovering by the snack table, hoping for a glimpse of Mariana, while Brody tries to make you laugh. Or complains about your classmates.

You tug on your tie. You can't tell if you got it too tight, or if ties are always supposed to make you feel like you're choking.

Brody's own tie is off-kilter, and his suit doesn't quite fit. It's too small around his shoulders. Out on the floor, Farshid's suit fits his own solid frame. You catch some of the other girls smiling at him, talking to him as he and Hope dance. You wish they'd look at you that way.

Mariana used to. Maybe she will again.

"Hey, guys," a raspy voice says. You didn't notice Reggie heading your way. He raises a fist. Brody's suit bunches at the shoulder as he raises his own fist to meet Reggie's.

You reflexively bump Reggie's fist, too, even though he still owes you twenty dollars. Even though in class, he acted like he had nothing to do with what you did. Like he didn't dare you to.

And the one time you called him on it, he just said, "I thought you knew I was joking!"

You kind of hate him.

And you hate seeing him and Brody so friendly. Brody's your best friend. He's supposed to be on your side, isn't he?

"Who'd you come with?" Brody asks.

Reggie shrugs. "Thought I'd see who I could score here."

Score. Like it's some sort of sport. Gross.

Reggie and Brody keep talking about the girls here, but you ignore them, scanning the gym for Mariana again. You don't know if she even came. If she ever asked anyone. But you thought you overheard her talking about it in German, so you have to hope.

A fist presses into your shoulder, a soft punch to get your attention.

"What?" you ask, turning back.

Reggie says, "You struck out, too?"

You didn't strike out—Brody accidentally sabotaged you.

But Brody chuckles. "He's got a thing for Mariana Herrera."

"Oh, really?" Reggie grins. He's got overly large canines for his face, which is angular with a forehead that takes up more than half of it. He's pasty white, and brown-haired, and kind of plain, if you're being honest.

You shake your head, look back out into the crowd, and then you spot her.

Mariana.

She's in a pretty blue dress that really shows off her . . . well, her beauty. And she is beautiful. She's talking with Hope Wang, who still has her arm looped through Farshid's.

On the one hand, you don't feel like dealing with Farshid, who's got to be the worst grudge-holder in the world. On the other, this might be your chance.

You glance back, hoping Brody might go with you to be your wingman, to apologize, but he and Reggie are still huddled up. You're on your own.

You straighten your shoulders and start walking, but then you wonder if your arms are swinging too much. They feel weird in the suit. Do your arms always move like that? You try to project confidence and saunter over.

But what's a saunter anyway? Are you doing it right?

You don't have time to figure it out. Suddenly you're there, right in front of Mariana. And Hope. And Farshid, who looks as nervous as you feel.

"Uh. Hey, Mariana." Your armpits feel sweaty all of a sudden, even though all the gym doors are open to get some airflow. Does it show?

"Hey," she says, but those shutters behind her eyes are still closed.

"Hey, Hope. Hey, Farshid."

Hope nods, but Farshid doesn't react. He hasn't even looked at you.

Annoyance bubbles in your stomach, but this isn't about him, this is about Mariana.

"Uh, I wondered if you wanted to dance?" you ask. "Mariana, I mean."

But Mariana glances past you, toward the wall where you'd left Brody and Reggie. Her lips press together as she looks back at you.

"No, thank you," she says softly.

"Oh." Now you wish you'd never come up here. You wish you would sweat so much it would carve a hole in the gym floor the way a river carves a canyon. That way you could disappear into it and never have to show your face again.

You should leave. She said no. She doesn't owe you anything. You know that.

But you can't stop yourself blurting out, "Why?"

"I'd hate to leave you with *blue balls* again," she says, and your face explodes in flames.

Farshid makes a little choking sound, and you hate him for that. You hate him for everything.

You want to wind back time and stop yourself from ever coming to this dance in the first place.

Instead you retreat, hands stuffed into your pockets to keep your arms from swinging.

"Struck out again?" Brody asks.

"You said you were gonna help me."

"You looked like you had it under control. Sorry."

"Yeah. Well." What could Brody have done anyway?

"Don't worry about that—" Reggie says a horrible word. Every part of you turns to ice. No, steam. No, ice.

"Don't call her that," you spit.

Reggie raises his hands. "Just saying, my guy."

"I'm not your guy." You turn on your heel and head for the doors. You wonder if you can get your mom to come get you. Or your dad. Or beg Marshall to leave early, but that's a losing proposition. You spotted him dancing super close with Lex earlier.

Brody grabs your arm, pulling you up short, but he lets go right away.

"What was that?"

"Reggie's a jerk." You grind your jaw. He's more than a jerk, but you can't say what you really think of him, not with chaperones in earshot. "He never even paid me that twenty dollars."

Brody laughs. "That was last semester. Forgive and forget."

Forgive? He never even said he was sorry. He never took accountability.

"Come on, man. You said we'd go stag together. You can't ditch me now." Brody bites his lower lip.

He's right. You can't ditch him.

"Fine. I'll stay. But we're ditching Reggie. Deal?"

Brody cracks a grin. "Deal."

ON MONDAY, YOU ASK FRAU IF YOU CAN SWITCH TO AN OPEN SEAT toward the front of the class, so you don't have to sit by Mariana.

You hate being in the front row, hate all the eyes on you as you raise your hand to get Pluspunkte, but whatever. Anything's better than the awkwardness.

After acing another quiz—this time on accusative articles—and working through a set of dialogues, you pack your backpack and head to history.

History, which is its own kind of awkward, since you sit right behind Farshid, who saw your utter humiliation.

You hate him for that.

You sit through Ms. Suchecki's lecture on the 1920s and the stock market crash and the Great Depression, but you only half listen. You keep thinking about the dance. About Mariana. And Reggie. And Brody. You stare at the back of Farshid's neck, which is brown, and smooth, and thick. You can actually see the muscles that connect it to his shoulders. Maybe Brody was right: Maybe he is a bit of a freak.

That doesn't stop the girls liking him, though. You even saw Mariana ask him for a dance, and he did, blushing the whole time, and you hate him for that.

You hate how he looks like a man and you look like a breadstick.

And you hate how small he makes you feel every time he looks at you. Not because you're not some sort of weird teenaged bodybuilder like him, but because he'll never let go of what you said back in September. That word, that one word, that you didn't even mean. But that doesn't matter to him. He thinks he's so perfect. He thinks he's never made a mistake.

"Dayton?" Ms. Suchecki calls your name. Crap, crap, crap. You're supposed to be reading aloud now, but you lost your spot.

"Black Tuesday," Farshid mutters, and you find the paragraph he's talking about, and you hate him for that, too. That he managed that small kindness. Like he thinks he's so much better than you.

He's not.

"SO," MS. SUCHECKI SAYS NEAR THE END OF CLASS. "LET'S TALK about your World War Two projects."

Soft groans ripple through the room. Ms. Suchecki only ever assigns partner projects, and last semester, for your project on the American Civil War, you had to do all the work yourself, because Ryder was completely useless.

Ms. Suchecki pulls a beat-up Royals cap from her desk, already filled with folded scraps of paper. "You know the drill. Pull a number. Whoever you match with is your partner."

The hat makes its way down the rows. Some people dig, like if they search hard enough, they can get matched up with a friend. It doesn't seem to work, though.

The cap reaches Farshid. He pulls out a slip. "Fourteen?" he says, quiet, like he's embarrassed by it.

No one says anything. No one else has pulled fourteen yet. The cap snakes its way down the row and back to you. You reach in and grab the first one you can, praying it's not a five, which is what Ryder pulled.

Except it's even worse.

You unfold your paper and stare at the number written in blue felt-tip ink.

Fourteen.

PART 4

march

20

FARSHID

YOU'VE NOTICED LATELY THAT IF YOU CLENCH YOUR FIST AND TURN your wrist a certain way, there's this vein that pops up on your forearm. Your arm gains still aren't where you want them to be, but this feels like a step in the right direction.

The door at the top of the stairs cracks open, and your mom shouts down.

"Farshid, are you almost done?"

"Almost," you tell her, relaxing your hand and grabbing the vacuum cord so you don't run over it (again).

Almost might be stretching the truth a bit. The basement is a mess, and for maybe the first time, it's not your fault.

Your LEGO collection is long-since packed up, in plastic tubs neatly stacked in the storage room. Your dad asked if you wanted to sell your collection, a suggestion that horrified you, though you're not sure why exactly, because it's not like you're going to play with them anymore, you're too old for LEGO sets now. They might be worth something someday, though.

But if you're being honest, there were times when it felt like those little minifigures were your only friends. A world of your own you could escape to. You know you're never going back to that world, but you're not ready to say goodbye, not yet.

Not even for some money, which, truth be told, you could use, because your gloves have worn out again, and worse than the wear is the smell. No matter how many little deodorizer pouches you stuff into them, you can't get it to go away. It smells like the school locker room, and wet dog, and you're not even sure what else. But it's bad.

You didn't know your own hands could smell so gross.

"Farshid!" Jina shouts from the bottom of the stairs.

You turn the vacuum off. "What?"

"Where did you put my nail polish?"

Without the LEGO fort occupying the basement, your sister has taken over part of it, turning it into some sort of nail salon for her and her friends when they hang out. The basement's not super well-ventilated, though, and you're starting to think the fumes have been getting to her.

You're still not sure why you're in charge of the basement this year instead of her, except force of habit, since as long as you can remember, the basement was your task. Even when you were really small and you mostly had to pick up your toys so one of your parents could vacuum.

Spring cleaning is a serious deal in your house, like it is in most Persian households as you get ready for Naw-Rúz. It's not like you're having company or anything; you don't have any family here, and the big Naw-Rúz party will be at the Bahá'í Center. Still, it's tradition, and your parents love their traditions.

Including making you clean the basement, even though you didn't mess it up (this time).

You point Jina toward the corner, where you stacked as much of her stuff as you could, nail polish and cotton balls and lotions and glitter and all that stuff that she suddenly seemed to not only want but know how to use, around the same time she stopped wanting to be seen with you in public. The bottles clink ominously in their boxes as she starts unstacking everything, making a brand-new mess for you to clean up.

You don't tell her off, though. She's your ride this afternoon, and if you don't stay in her good graces, you'll have to ask Maman instead, and you'd rather swallow one of those bottles of nail polish than be stuck in a car with your mother as she interrogates you about what friend you're visiting (not a friend), what the project's on (you haven't decided yet), will you be eating there (doubtful since the macros will be way off), and when you want to go clothes shopping for Naw-Rúz (never, at least not with her, because you're too old to go clothes shopping with your mom anymore).

"Farshid!" Jina shouts again.

You stifle a sigh and turn off the vacuum again. You think you've vacuumed the same spot like three times now, because you keep getting interrupted.

"Yeah?"

"Can you be ready in an hour?"

If she stops making more messes.

"Sure."

DAYTON'S HOUSE ISN'T THAT FAR AWAY FROM YOURS. TWO MILES, tops. You could run it, honestly, if you didn't mind showing up sweaty and winded from the big hill along the way. You never knew he lived so close. You've never been to his house before.

Truth be told, you've put this project off longer than you

should've. Ms. Suchecki assigned it back in February, but now it's March, and you still haven't touched it, haven't even talked to Dayton about it, even though you told Ms. Suchecki you didn't mind being his partner when she pulled you aside after class to double-check.

You didn't *want* to be partnered with him, of course, but you couldn't say no, because if you complained about it, people would definitely read into it, and you don't want anyone reading into it, so you just said it was fine, as everyone filed out of the classroom around you, and Dayton eyed you like he knew you and Ms. Suchecki were talking about him.

And now here you are, outside his house. It's painted a vivid pumpkin kind of orange, which you didn't know houses could actually be outside of, like, a Disney movie.

"Let us know when you need picking up," Jina says. She's in the driver's seat, and Baba's in the passenger seat, because she's still getting in her practice hours before she can take her actual test.

"Okay," you say, but you don't get out of the car. Your arm feels leaden, and not just because you did two back-to-back classes and an hour of weights this morning, all before coming home and cleaning up the basement.

You don't want to do this. You don't want to be here.

But you definitely don't want to be at home, either, because there's no way you were going to invite Dayton to work at your house, not with the haft-seen in the entryway, and pictures of your family back in Iran on the walls, and a framed portrait of 'Abdu'l-Bahá on the piano. You don't want to have to explain who you are to him, because Dayton might just turn around and use it against you.

He's done it before.

But you can't tell anyone that, least of all him, so when he pestered you because you only had a week left to finish your project, you finally agreed to this.

And now you're standing in front of his door, ringing the bell, as Jina pulls away from the curb a little too quickly and you could swear you hear Baba telling her to *take it easy, it's not a race*. You cling to the straps of your backpack. Should you have brought something? It's not like you're a dinner guest, though. And you didn't avoid having him over to see your Persian household only to show off being Persian by arriving with a plate of shirini covered in Saran Wrap.

"Hey," Dayton says when the door swings open. He's dressed in a teal KC Current shirt and black gym shorts, the kind that hang down to his knees. Your own shorts are cut higher, to show off your quads, which are the only part of you that feels A-tier. Well, that and your glutes, which is probably genetic, because you once overheard Maman telling Jina that big butts run in Persian families.

"Hey." Your own faded Magic: The Gathering shirt is feeling a little tight, like can't-quite-move tight instead of make-your-gains-pop tight, but Saturday is your laundry day, so you were mostly out of clean clothes. "Thanks for having me."

"Sure." Dayton's still standing in the doorway, though, looking at you, blue eyes catching the sunlight.

You wonder if he'd look less weird if he wasn't a bigot. If being ugly inside makes people ugly outside. If he even is ugly, or if you just tell yourself that because of what you know about him. His skin is smooth, and his hair is a nice golden color, and he looks like he doesn't have to shave yet, whereas you're up to three times a week now.

You ask, "Shoes on or off?" and Dayton startles and gets out of the way so you can step inside. Your house is definitely shoes off, but Dayton's got his own sneakers on still, even on the white carpet.

"It's fine either way," he answers, which isn't very useful, but you can hear Maman's voice chiding you to treat a stranger's home even better than your own, so you kneel to untie your tennis shoes and leave them—alone—near the door.

You wait for him to see if you want a drink or snacks or anything, so you can turn him down (well, water's fine, but snacks, no), but he doesn't. "I usually work in the dining room," he says instead, so you follow him. His house is weirdly similar to yours—the layout is basically the same, except he's got an extra closet in the hall where you've got a toilet, and the windows have extra little round bits at the top, and all the furniture is different.

Also, it doesn't smell like rice, the way home usually does. It doesn't smell like anything, actually, except something a little spicy, but then you realize as you follow Dayton that it's him that smells spicy. It's a nice spiciness, though. It honestly reminds you a little of Cooper, who always smells nice, too.

"What's that smell?" you ask before you can stop yourself.

"Hm?" He drops into his seat and opens his laptop. It's dented in the back and chipped by the charging port. "Oh. The new Burberry."

"The what?"

"Burberry? Cologne?"

"Oh." You feel yourself blushing. Should *you* be wearing cologne? Baba didn't talk to you about that. He's talked to you about shaving and deodorant and *hormones* and a bunch of other things about *being a young man*, but cologne wasn't one of them.

Maybe it's an American thing. Maybe it's just another thing all the other boys know that you don't get to know. Because you're an immigrant. Because you're . . .

You can't think that. Not here. Not with Dayton right across from you.

So you say, "Cool." And you pull out your own laptop and history notebook. "Where should we start?"

21
DAYTON

YOU REALLY HATE GROUP PROJECTS.

You've hated them since the first one you did in sixth grade. You and three classmates had to do a presentation on blowing the biggest dish soap bubbles. But you're the only one who actually did any work; everyone else just goofed off blowing bubbles.

Technically, this is more of a partner project than a group project. It's just you and Farshid.

You still hate it.

You can't believe you got partnered with him.

Farshid's quiet as you work, his head bowed so his dark hair hangs down and covers his face. He talked a little, earlier, as you settled on doing a presentation on the Tehran Conference. A few times he said *Tehran* with a bit of an accent, but when you asked him if that's how it's really pronounced, he got quiet again and just said, "Never mind."

Farshid's voice has gotten deeper. You wonder if it's changing or if he's doing that on purpose, the way Brody does sometimes if there are girls around.

Either way, it makes you hate him more. The girls in class keep looking at him. Smiling at him. Talking about him.

When he runs a hand through his hair and scratches his head, his bicep and forearm flex. It's not like Brody, who does it on purpose. Farshid's just in ridiculous shape.

You're still a breadstick, but you don't want to spend half your life in the gym, like Farshid the Freak.

Maybe you should, though. Apparently it's working for him.

"Whatever happened with you and Hope anyway?" you suddenly ask, and feel a rotten thrill when Farshid looks up, alarmed, and then down again. You know through the grapevine that they never hooked up again after the Sweetheart Dance.

Maybe he said something messed up, too. Grossed her out.

Pulled a Brody.

Farshid shrugs and keeps looking down, though his voice pitches back up. "We're just friends."

"I heard she asked you out and you turned her down."

Another glance up at you, longer this time, and you think his cheeks get darker. His skin is brown and doesn't blush like yours, a crimson flush that can be seen from space, but you're pretty sure he's blushing.

He shrugs. "I didn't like her like that."

"Why? She's hot." You picture Brody, wondering aloud how Farshid managed to hook up with her in the first place. As if he didn't know all the girls talked about Farshid's looks. As if he hadn't started lifting more to try and keep up.

"Can we just focus on the project?" Farshid scowls and turns back to his computer, but his face is definitely turning a reddish brown, and his nostrils are flaring, and something in you won't let it go, not until you get a real rise out of him.

"I'm just saying. You totally fumbled the ball."

Farshid mutters something.

"What?"

He sighs and looks back up, his dark eyebrows drawn to a point. "I said, she's not a ball. She's a person. Maybe if you and your friends didn't treat all the girls so bad, you could get a date yourself."

"Dates are for losers," you say, even though it stings, because you *almost* had a date. Would have, if Brody hadn't accidentally sabotaged you. But Brody apologized for that. And Farshid's here in front of you, acting like he's better than you.

But he's not.

"Whatever," Farshid says again. He pulls his notes closer, but that tightness in your stomach won't go away. You grab his notebook out of his hands.

"What is wrong with you?" he asks, and a thrill of fear seizes your spine, because he's a lot bigger than you, you just forgot that for the moment because he was hunched over. He's always so quiet, it honestly didn't occur to you that he could beat you up if he wanted to.

But you're all fired up now.

"Nothing. What's wrong with *you*? We're supposed to be working together and you barely talk."

"Maybe I don't have much to say to you." Farshid crosses his arms. They *are* rather large. But he can't actually do anything, not in your house. He's stuck here—you're both stuck here—and you're so sick and tired of everyone, *everyone*, treating you like crap.

"Seriously, how long are you going to punish me for something I did last year?" You toss his notebook back at him, but it misses and sails over his shoulder. "You're such a bully."

Farshid's jaw drops. "*I'm* a bully? You're the one who . . ."

You wait for him to say it, but he gets this look in his face, like he's going to be sick, and that just makes you mad.

"I said I was sorry, dude. I got punished. What more do you want?"

"I don't know," he says. "You act like saying you're sorry was supposed to fix everything. But I haven't seen you at RC. I haven't seen you making amends. I haven't even seen you tell Brody to stop being such a jerk to everyone."

That's not fair at all. Brody's a good guy. "Brody's not—"

"You don't want forgiveness. You don't want to make things better. You just want people to forget what you did."

That's not true. You took accountability. You wrote that apology note. And why would Farshid expect you at RC? That's for performative jerks like Cooper, who'd rather look good than actually do good.

"You don't know me. You don't know what I want." You kind of wish you *were* in a boxing ring. Yeah, you'd lose, but maybe you could land a few punches at least. Maybe that would make you feel better. Right now, all you can do is shout.

"And why are you so mad anyway? I didn't even do anything to you!"

"You don't get it, do you? You did it to *everyone*. All of us. And you act like you're the victim. You act like it was just one word, like it doesn't matter, but it does. You have no idea what it's like. You have no idea how it feels to go to school every day and have everyone talking about you behind your back."

"Are you kidding? *Everyone* talks about me behind my back."

"It's not the same!" Farshid shouts. "They're doing it because of what you *did*, not who you *are*. You don't have to be afraid, you don't have to wonder if people know you're—"

Farshid's voice cuts out with a choking sound. Like someone punched him in the throat. But there's no one here, just the two of you, glaring across the table, breathing hard. Farshid's eyes are wide, and he looks like he's going to explode, flip the table or maybe smash it in two.

He lurches away so fast he knocks over his chair. He grabs his laptop. Scoops his notebook off the ground. Stuffs everything into his backpack and fights with the zipper as he stomps to the entryway to stuff his feet into his shoes.

"Where are you going?"

"Home," he says. His voice has gone soft now. Shaky and low.

"You can't just walk."

"It's only a few miles."

"But . . ."

You don't know what you expected, but not this. Not him running away.

"What about the project?"

He yanks his shoelaces so tight you're surprised he doesn't slice off his own foot. But then he's standing again, and you didn't mean to get so close, because now you're basically chest to chest. And you know he's bigger and taller than you, but something about him seems so small right now.

Small and afraid.

Afraid of . . . you?

He opens his mouth, but nothing comes out. He just shakes his head, yanks the door open, and runs. Down your driveway, out onto the sidewalk, arms slicing, legs flying, like he runs every day. He probably does.

You watch him go, and all that fire you felt, all that righteous anger at him being such a jerk to you for so many months, drains away.

You're not even sure you were actually angry. Maybe you were just sad. Is that what this hollow inside you is?

Yeah. You're sad.

And now you made him sad, too. Sad and afraid.

What does he have to be afraid of, anyway?

You don't have to wonder if people know you're—

Oh.

Oh no.

Maybe you *did* do something to him. Maybe you did the worst possible thing you could've done to him.

Maybe he has every right to be afraid of you.

Maybe you're a bad guy after all.

22

FARSHID

YOUR HEART IS POUNDING, HALF FROM THE PACE YOU'VE SET yourself, half because you can't believe what you almost said.

Did Dayton catch it? Did he know what you were about to say?

Did you stop yourself in time?

You don't know. You don't know.

You don't know.

He could tell everyone.

You pace yourself faster, like you can outrun all the voices if you just get your speed up. Your feet pound the sidewalk. You're in your boxing shoes, heavy and flat and solid on the bottom, good for doing squats or hitting the heavy bag but not for running, and you feel every single jolt as your feet hit the sidewalk.

Your eyes are burning, starting to blur. You tell yourself it's the sun, not the dread scooping out your chest like your dad scoops out the sweet and sour pulp of a passionfruit.

You tell yourself that, but it doesn't work.

You can lie to everyone else, but you can't keep lying to yourself. It doesn't work anymore. The truth is inside, growing and growing, no matter how you try to ignore it, stuff it down, put it in the corner tucked away where no one will ever find it.

Everyone already thinks you're different for being Iranian. For being an immigrant. For being Bahá'í. What would they say if they knew you were . . .

You still can't say the word, not even in the safety of your own mind. All you can do is feel out the space around it, the jagged edges poised to rip your world apart if you aren't careful.

You don't want this.

So you keep running. You fly down the big hill, sprint back up the next, savoring the burn in your legs, your lungs, because anything is better than the burning in your heart, your soul, because no matter how fast you run you can never outrun that word.

That one word.

THE HOUSE IS QUIET WHEN YOU GET HOME, SWEAT-SLICKED, breathing hard. Your pulse pounds in your ears. Your hair sticks to your forehead and neck. The wind has picked up, and clouds are rolling in, maybe the spring rain Baba has been hoping for, since his garden needs it. But Baba's gone, probably still practicing driving with Jina, who hasn't had to drive in the rain yet. You hope she freaks out less about the rain than she did about the highway at nighttime. You weren't with her, but you feel like you were, you've heard Baba tell the story so many times.

You kick your shoes off. Peel your hair off your forehead. Pull your sweat-drenched shirt off to try and dry your face, your chest, that spot on your lower back that always leaves a gross oval at the bottom of your shirts. You catch a glance at yourself in the hallway mirror, and you're still scrawnier than you want to be, you still haven't gotten the gains you need, you still have that sunken spot in your chest, you're still soft and weak and scared.

You squeeze your eyes shut. You don't know what's going to happen at school on Monday. What Dayton will do, who he'll tell, what misery he's planning to make your life even worse.

You think you're going to be sick, but you swallow and swallow until it stops feeling like your protein shake is on its way back up. Your tongue feels too big for your mouth.

You stretch against the kitchen counter, chug a glass of water, take the stairs slowly, one at a time, because your legs are feeling a little wobbly since you didn't warm up before you sprinted out of Dayton's house, and you didn't account for the extra cardio in your meal planning for today.

You pull your phone out to add in the extra run, to figure out how many calories you need to add to maintain your progress, your head down and distracted when you step into your room, which is why you don't realize you're not alone until your mom says, "Farshid?"

You don't scream. Screaming is for little kids.

But you *do* let out a cry of alarm, because you didn't expect her to be there, pulling a pair of boxers out from beneath your bed and adding them to the laundry basket.

"Maman!" you shout.

"Farshid-jan, don't startle me like that!" she says in Farsi, but you stick to English.

"What are you doing? I told you to stay out of my room!"

"You said you needed to do laundry today," she says. "Why are you home so soon?"

"I told you I'd do it myself!" What is wrong with her? Why doesn't she ever listen to you? You told her you'd do your laundry.

You don't want her going through your sweaty gym clothes, much less your sleep clothes, because sometimes you've woken up and felt weird and you know what that means, and to be honest, most times you've been awake when you made the mess, and God, please don't let her have noticed that, and—

"I was just trying to help." Your mother sets down the laundry basket and crosses her arms. "You don't need to have such an attitude."

"And *you* don't need to be going into my room when I've told you not to!" You don't realize you're flailing until the wet shirt is already flying across the room, smacking against the wall beneath the poster you got at the last Magic prerelease tournament when you came in second. "I deserve privacy!"

"It's just some laundry," she says. "And you said you'd be out late. What are you doing home, anyway? What about your project?"

"It's fine," you say, crossing your arms over your chest, because you're cooling off now, and you don't want your mother looking at your chest anyway, your pecs aren't nearly as developed as you want them to be, and your core is still lacking definition.

"But you said it was thirty percent of your grade."

She's talking to you like you're a child.

"God, Maman, it's fine, okay? I'll finish it later."

"Why are you shouting at me? I'm just asking!" She raises her voice now. Your mother doesn't raise her voice very often. "I don't know what's going on with you, but I'm tired of you taking it out on me."

"Well, I'm tired of you snooping through my room and getting into my business!"

"You're my *son*," she says. "*You* are my business. Why are you so upset with me? Is it about Hope?"

No, it's not about a girl, even if she was nice, because you were never anything more than friends with her, though you did feel like crap turning her down when she asked you on a real date. You should've just said yes, should've kissed her on the lips instead of the cheek after Sweetheart, should've slow danced and fast danced and whatever kind of dance would let people know you *do* like her, like girls, like that, instead of being a coward.

"No, it's not about her, it's not about anything. Would you just leave me alone?" Your voice is hoarse, cracking in the middle, and you're cracking, too, because everything inside you is swirling, about to burst, and you can't handle it.

You can't.

But your mother won't leave you alone. Instead she reaches for you. You back away, and she flares her nostrils, and finally she snaps and shouts, "Why won't you tell me what's going on?"

And you snap, too, splitting like a dry old twig, as you shout back, "Because if I do you won't love me!"

Maman reels back, like you've caught her with a cross to the jaw.

No, she just steps back, hand over her heart, like you stabbed her in it. She presses her lips together and takes another step away from you, and the backs of her knees hit your bed and she sits with a soft cry.

You don't know why you said that.

You don't know why you do anything anymore.

But your mother is crying now, and you're crying, too, hot fat tears that sting your cheeks.

You didn't mean to make her cry.

You're sorry, but your throat is tied in a knot, so you can't say it. All you can do is cry yourself.

Your mom clears her throat and blinks. She takes a deep breath and looks up at you, and you want to shrink away from her eyes, because even now they're full of nothing but kindness.

Persian has lots of poetic ways of telling someone you love them. *You are my soul.* Or *I'd become a sacrifice for you.* Or even *I'll eat your liver.*

But your mom says it in English instead:

"I love you."

Your heart squeezes tight, so hard you think you might double over, but you try to breathe.

"I will always love you. Your father and I crossed an ocean for the love of you, maman. Why would you ever think I'd stop?"

You cry harder now, because you know she and Baba gave up everything they knew—their lives, their families, their friends, their *home*—when they left Iran. And they did it for you and Jina and Nadeem. Because they love you.

Your mother stands again, steps in close, and when you don't back off, she pulls you into a hug. You're taller than her—you have been since last year—but this is the first time you've noticed just how much. You could rest your chin on her head if you wanted to, but you don't want to. You wish you were small again, small enough that her hugs felt like they were the whole world, like you didn't need to breathe as long as you were in her arms.

But you hug her back, hard, and that tightness in your heart moves up into your throat. You can't tell her.

You can't.

You can't tell anyone.

You don't want it to be true.

But you don't want to make your mother cry, either.

"Azizam," she says. "It's okay."

You shake your head. It's not okay.

But something in you bubbles up. And before you can clamp your mouth shut, before you can stop yourself, before you can call the words back, you tell her.

23
DAYTON

YOU'RE NERVOUS MONDAY MORNING, DREAD POOLING IN YOUR stomach as you try to count up all the hours, minutes, seconds before you'll have to see Farshid again in history.

Is he still mad? Will he even talk to you? How are you supposed to do a project together after what happened?

Did he even make it home safely? You don't know how far away he lives from you. What if he tripped and fell and has been in a ditch since Saturday? What if you were the last one to see him alive? Would that make you a suspect? Is it even a crime? What do all the different degrees of murder mean anyway?

"You okay?" Marshall asks as he pulls into his spot.

"I'm fine."

"You've been weird all weekend."

"Have not."

You haven't been weird. You've just been thinking.

Wondering if Farshid was right and you haven't done nearly as much as you should have done to make up for *the incident*. Wondering if you've been the bad guy all along.

Wondering if it's too late to change things now.

"You ever think you're right about something and then realize you're wrong?" you blurt out.

"I'm your older brother. I'm never wrong."

You snort and shove him toward his door as you open your own. He gets out, too, grabs his backpack from the back seat, and looks at you over his car's trunk.

"For real, though?" he asks. "Yeah."

"What did you do?"

He shrugs. "Tried to do better. What else can you do?"

You don't know.

You thought you were doing better.

Now nothing makes sense.

You shrug. "Thanks, I guess."

YOU CAN'T DECIDE IF YOU'RE RELIEVED OR NOT WHEN YOU GET TO Ms. Suchecki's class and Farshid's already at his desk. His shoulders take up too much room, but he's hunched over, his head bowed over his notebook so his hair hides his face.

Still, when you take your seat, he straightens and looks right at you.

Not dead in a ditch, at least, but what now? Is he going to punch you right in the middle of class? There's something different about him, though. Something in his face, but you can't read it.

You swallow and wait, but he doesn't speak, so you have to. "You good?"

He blinks at you. Looks away, and then back again. "I wanted to apologize."

That's the last thing you expected, so you just blurt out, "Huh?"

You don't even correct yourself.

"I'm sorry," he clarifies. "For my behavior Saturday."

"Oh." You're grateful for your Burberry because your underarms suddenly feel wet, even though the air conditioner is finally going. "It's cool."

"Thanks. I was mad about some other stuff and took it out on you. I won't do it again." His voice is so soft you can barely make him out over the random noise of everyone taking their seats and pulling out their notebooks. "Maybe we can finish up our project after school today? We can work in the library or something?"

"Yeah. Okay."

Maybe he did fall into a ditch after all. Maybe he got a concussion or something. Why else would his personality do a complete one-eighty? Or maybe he's scared of you. Maybe he thinks you know something about him, something he doesn't want other people to know, and are going to use it against him.

But then again, maybe he really is genuinely sorry for how he acted.

You know what it's like, losing your head, saying things you don't mean to.

The bell rings before you can say anything else, so you have to sit there in silence, trying to figure out what just happened.

Of all the ways you imagined today going, this was not it.

"WHAT'RE YOU DOING AFTER SCHOOL TODAY?" BRODY ASKS AS YOU jog along the track. With the weather so nice, you're outside today, getting warmed up for flag football.

"Finishing up my history project."

"I thought you did that this weekend?"

You don't want to tell him about your fight, so you just say, "We did, but we didn't get it all done."

Brody blows a raspberry. "Oh man. I got this new game, it's like *Fortnite* except you're a wizard, and you can even do split screen so you can play with a friend."

"Sorry." That does sound fun, even though you're terrible at shooters. "I'd rather be doing that than homework, I promise."

You hate having to ditch Brody. But your project is a big chunk of your grade.

"Later this week?"

"Bet." Brody's eyes slide past you, across the big oval of the track, to the opposite side, where Farshid and Cooper are running side by side. Farshid doesn't even look out of breath. You wonder how many miles he runs each day.

Couldn't be you.

"I can't believe you got stuck with him for your project," Brody says. "Did he do anything weird at yours?"

"What does that even mean?"

"I don't know, he's just . . . you know, super sus."

"He's fine," you say, surprising yourself.

But then, he did say he was sorry. Not for everything, but for last weekend at least. He even offered to stay after school to finish the project, when he could've just given up and made you do it all. Or let your grade tank.

He tried to make things right. A little bit, at least.

And if he is *sus*, or gay, or . . . well, anything?

You're not going to be the one to tell Brody.

"If you say so," Brody huffs.

"Don't worry," you assure him. "You're still my best friend."

You're not sure you've ever actually said that to him before. Not out loud. But he deserves to know. He hasn't been perfect—then again, neither have you—but he's been there for you, which is more than you can say for anyone else.

Brody makes a face. "Gay," he teases, but then he turns serious. "You're my best friend, too, man. For real."

24

FARSHID

"WE MISSED YOU YESTERDAY." NOUR HANDS YOU A PIECE OF Scotch tape from the roll, even though she has a collection of strips dangling from the tip of each finger, like inverted fingernails.

You stick the poster for next week's Movie Nite to the wall and shrug, not because you didn't miss her (and Cooper) but because you're not sure why it's spelled *Nite* in the first place. You're also not sure why you—well, the RC—is doing *The Babadook* in March, instead of in October, which would make more sense. And now that you think of it, you're *also* not sure what makes it queer cinema in the first place.

You're coming to terms with that word, even if you haven't told anyone other than Maman. And Baba. And Nadeem and Jina. And you only told everyone else because Baba and Jina came home while you were still crying and hugging Maman and she was telling you it was okay, and then you told Nadeem on Sunday because it felt weird to leave him out. But you haven't mentioned anything at school, not even to Nour. You don't think you're scared. Well, not *that* scared.

Nothing feels as scary as it had been telling Maman, even though now that it's done you're not sure why you were so scared to begin with. You're not scared anymore, but you don't know if you want to deal with it, at least not yet. Not for a while.

So instead of saying something at RC, you just kept quiet and volunteered to help Nour put up posters for (misspelled) Movie Nite.

"I missed you, too," you say. "But at least me and Dayton finished our presentation."

It took another two hours of work, mostly in silence, but now it's finished and you don't have to spend any one-on-one time with Dayton ever again. Well, unless you count actually giving the presentation, in which case you'll be one-on-one with him at the front of the class, but Ms. Suchecki will be there at her desk, and the rest of the class will all be out in front of you, and it's only an eight-minute presentation anyway.

"You missed all the drama," she says, following you down the hall until you find another good spot for a poster. "Guess who broke up?"

"I don't know." You're not even sure you could say who in RC was dating. "Who?"

Nour mentions two juniors, both white girls, one with blue hair and one with green hair, and truth be told you never could tell the two of them apart because they were basically inseparable, but you're grateful to have Nour talking, because that means you don't have to.

You don't feel anxious, at least you don't think you do, but you do feel quiet. This new normal still feels strange and alien and fragile, yet this part, Nour talking about everyone else's drama, is familiar.

"—go yesterday anyway?"

"What?" you ask, taping up a poster next to the water bottle–filling station, but high up enough it won't get splashed by people being clumsy with their bottles. You missed most of what Nour said.

She snorts and hands you more tape. "I said, how'd it go yesterday anyway?"

You blink at her.

"With Dayton."

"Oh. Fine." You shrug. After you apologized, he seemed . . . subdued, maybe. Or at least a little quiet. He didn't bother you about Hope anymore. Didn't bother you about anything. Just focused on getting your slides in the right order, and thankfully he didn't insist on doing them in Papyrus, because that might've been another fight actually.

But Nour shakes her head. "I can't believe you got stuck with him."

You shrug. Yeah, it wasn't great, but you're tired of running, and you realized something yesterday:

You're bigger than him.

Not just physically (though you definitely are), but inside, too, like you could feel him shrinking away from you, and it's weird but some small part of you feels a little bit sorry for him.

Just a little bit.

You don't know how to explain any of that, though, so you just say, "He wasn't as bad as I thought."

Nour's eyebrows shoot up so high they nearly launch themselves off her face. "Are we talking about the same Dayton here? The one that shouted a slur in the middle of an assembly? And then wrote it across our board when no one was watching?"

"I don't think that was him. The board, I mean." You've seen his handwriting. "I'm not saying I *like* him, just that he could've been worse."

Yeah, he shouted that word at the beginning of the year, but as far as you know he hasn't said it again, so you're still mad at him but not as mad as you would be if he kept doing it. Then again, he's still friends with Brody, who you're pretty sure *does* use that word, and often, if the frequency of *no homos* is any indication.

So, no. You don't like Dayton, and you're certainly not going to forgive or forget. You meant what you told him, that he's never really done anything to make things right. But he hasn't done anything to make them worse, either. He seems to hope everyone will just forget it sooner or later.

You can't decide what that makes him.

Nour looks like she's sucking on a lemon wedge. "I still don't like him."

"Same," you say.

You don't think you hate him anymore. He could've told everyone what you said—what you didn't say—but he didn't. That's something, right?

You don't hate him, but you definitely don't like him, either.

YOUR PROTEIN BAR IS CHEWY AND TASTELESS BUT STILL BETTER than the weird chemical-y taste of the protein shakes your dad bought you from Costco last time you asked for some. Better than the brownies at the RC meeting, too, not in the taste department because you didn't taste them, but because the protein bar won't throw off your macros.

You're grateful you don't have to do the Nineteen-Day Fast for another year, because missing meals and snacks from dawn to dusk would definitely interfere with your gains.

Truth be told, you're not sure you'll do it next year. You're not sure you feel all that Bahá'í, especially with being . . . well. Gay. The teachings aren't super on board with that, even though Maman and Baba promised you could still be Bahá'í if you wanted to.

You're not sure you want to. You're still figuring out what it means to be . . . gay.

It feels strange and frightening and liberating to think the word, even if you don't say it, not even at RC, where they talk about how beautiful it is to be out, how the world is made better by people being their true selves.

You're not even sure who your true self is yet. You think you might need a while to figure it out.

The door opens behind you; you turn as Cooper comes to join you on the sidewalk. The wind has picked up, blowing in puffy gray clouds from the west, and it wafts his fragrance your way. Your mouth goes dry, and you nearly choke on your protein bar as you swallow it down.

"H-hey," you manage.

"Hey." His brown hands grip the straps of his backpack. "You okay?"

"Me?"

You know he's got to be talking to you. He's *looking* at you, and there's no one else around waiting for pickup. But what is he seeing that would make him ask something like that?

"I'm good. Why?"

"You just seem quiet is all."

Well, you've had a lot on your mind the past few days, but you can't tell him that. Or can you? He's in RC after all, and you're still not sure exactly why. Maybe he's an ally like Nour, but maybe he's like you.

Your skin tingles at the thought; excitement thrills up your spine, tinged with fear, too.

"Just thinking," you tell him, but you can feel your cheeks heating as he looks at you. You stuff the rest of your protein bar in your mouth to give yourself an excuse not to talk, except now you have a slightly sticky plastic wrapper in your hand, so you follow the sidewalk along the retaining wall to where there's a big black trash can.

Cooper follows you, matching his steps to yours. He really is handsome. He's not in your kind of shape, but he looks good exactly the way he is, and he smells amazing, like Persian tea, like warm spices, like springtime.

"You always smell nice," you tell him.

He smiles wide, showing off the little gap in his teeth again. You hope he never has to get braces, because they would ruin his smile.

"Thanks," he says. "I just switched to my spring fragrance. It's D&G."

You don't know what that means, but who cares, because he smells like orange blossoms and almonds and happiness.

"You always look good. You must work out, like, a ton," he tells you.

Your face nearly catches fire, and your cheeks clench up as you try not to smile too big. You look down at your feet, because your chest feels tight and embarrassed, but he thinks you look good.

You're still working on some problem spots, but you're making progress, and he sees that. He sees it and thinks you look good.

He thinks you look good, and you think he looks good, and smells good, too, and you're both here, waiting for pickup after RC, and you feel brave (when did you get so brave?) so you just ask him.

"Would you ever want to, like, go out? Sometime? With me?"

You don't know where you would go or what you would do, but you don't think it would matter that much as long as it was with him. Just the two of you.

Cooper's smile does something then. It doesn't dim, but it does shift a bit. He scratches the back of his head.

"Oh. Sorry, man. I'm not . . ."

Oh no.

No no no no no.

"I was just—" you start, heat flaring in your cheeks, panic rising in your throat, choking you, but before you can say anything he rests a hand on your shoulder.

"It's cool. I'm honored you trusted me," he says. "Thank you."

Your pulse is still pounding in your ears, but he's not running away. Not making fun of you. He's just standing there, still, like he was before you asked.

"I like you as a friend," he says. "I hope this won't change that."

"Yeah. No. I mean. It won't." You swallow.

You can be friends with him. Can't you?

Yeah, he just totally rejected you. That's what this is, right? You asked him out.

You asked a boy out and he said no.

But he's your friend.

"We're cool," you say, even though you're not, but you hope you will be, when this ache between your ribs goes away.

You don't want him to stop being your friend. Even if he did turn you down.

Now you know what Hope must've felt like when you said no to her, told her you just wanted to be friends. You should've bought her chocolates or something to make up for it.

"Cool," he says, giving your shoulder a squeeze, then furrowing his brow. "Jeez, you're strong. What do you do?"

"Just boxing. And weights."

Plus running, and occasional kickboxing, and also your food plan and Coach Nico's cross-training, which is usually jumping onto boxes or doing burpees or whatever.

"And I watch my macros, so—"

A car pulls up, but it's not your dad's, and Cooper doesn't move, so it's not for him, either.

From the other side of the retaining wall, Brody Connors emerges, backpack slung off one shoulder, headphones around his neck. He gets into the red hatchback, but before it pulls away, he looks right at you, a crooked grin fixed on his face.

You feel cold all over, limbs frozen in place, lungs seized tight. Cooper says your name, but it sounds like he's far away, underwater.

"What?" you ask.

"You good?"

You're . . . not sure.

Did he hear you and Cooper?

Does he know?

Do you care? You're not sure. After all, your family knows, and they still love you, and Cooper knows, too, and yeah, he rejected you, but only for a date, not for being friends. And you know Nour would be fine if you told her, and you're not even sure why you didn't, except for inertia.

You thought it would be the end of the world if anyone found out what was really in your heart, but the sun is still shining, and the breeze is still blowing, and Cooper's still standing beside you.

"I'm good," you tell him.

And you think you might actually mean it.

25

DAYTON

YOU NEVER SHOULD'VE ACCEPTED THAT COFFEE. BUT IT WAS FREE after the Starbucks drive-through messed up Marshall's order and had to remake it. You didn't want it to go to waste.

You never liked coffee before. You're pretty sure you still don't, and never will. Still, with sugar and cream and caramel and chocolate and whatever else was in it, it tasted more like dessert than coffee.

You've had plenty of Coke before, but the caffeine in coffee hit you different. Made you feel weird and unsettled.

Made you have to pee, too.

Everything was fine in choir. ELA too. But halfway through German it hit you. Thank god Frau likes you and didn't give you grief when you asked for a hall pass.

You're fine now, except you think your hand might be shaking a little bit. And your mouth is dry. And it feels like you can smell your own coffee breath deep down in the back of your sinuses, like a cat making that weird face so it can smell things with the roof of its mouth.

You're so distracted trying to smell your own breath as you head back to Frau's class, you walk right past Brody hovering in a cross hall. You back up.

"Hey," you say. He's not alone. Reggie's with him, too, the both of them leaning against a locker. You can't tell if they have hall passes or not. Some teachers just give slips of paper or whatever, but not Frau.

Her hall pass is a plastic miniature of a helmet, the old-timey kind with the spike on top. The chin strap is looped around your wrist, which made washing your hands unwieldy.

Brody goes in for a fist bump, leaning away from the locker, and you realize it's covered in thick-point Sharpie. You can only make out the last three letters, but your breath catches.

"Brody . . . ," you warn.

"Be cool, man," Reggie says.

"It's just a joke," Brody adds. "Come on."

"It's not cool," you say. "It's not a joke."

You didn't know better when you shouted it out at a stranger, but you do now. You think of what Farshid said: that it makes people afraid.

You don't want people to be afraid of you. You don't want your classmates to be afraid at all.

"Why are you doing this?" you ask, because you honestly can't figure it out. Yeah, Brody's crass sometimes, and yeah, he's always "no homo" this, "no homo" that, but Brody's not a bad guy.

He's not.

He's doing a bad thing, though.

The hallway is cool, but your skin feels hot, like you've been in the sun too long and it's going to burn.

Brody leans in, a smile lighting his face. "Yesterday I heard Farshid ask out Cooper."

You blink.

You heard that wrong.

Right?

Cooper's straight. At least he was last time you checked, which, granted, was over the summer. Yeah, he and Farshid talk sometimes in conditioning, but wow. You don't know what to feel about all this. But still, that doesn't excuse them—

"Wait, is that Cooper's locker?"

"Nah, Farshid's." Reggie laughs, glancing both ways down the hall before turning back and going in for another layer of Sharpie. "I always thought he was sus. But for, like, being a terrorist, not for being gay."

"Stop!" you say, grabbing for Reggie's arm, throwing off his linework on the *T*.

"Cut it out, man," he says, yanking his arm away. Brody gets between you, gently maneuvering you away.

"Leave him alone," Brody says. "He's not hurting anyone."

"He's hurting Farshid."

"Come on, it's just a word," Brody says. "And what does it matter? You hate the guy. We all do."

You don't hate Farshid.

You don't like him, but that doesn't mean you hate him. It doesn't mean you want to hurt him.

"It doesn't matter. It's wrong." You clear your throat. "If you don't stop, I'm going to . . ."

But stop what? It's too late. It's already there, even if the letters aren't all filled in yet.

"You'll what?" Reggie asks. "You gonna tell on us? Who's gonna believe you anyway? Everyone knows you hate the gays."

You should tell.

Tell on Reggie, at least. He was the one who put you up to it at the assembly, after all. And you remember that word on the whiteboard before Thanksgiving. Back then you wondered if it was him, but now . . .

What about Brody, though?

Brody's your friend.

Brody doesn't mean it, does he?

You shake your head and turn away. Your shoe squeaks against the tile floor. Brody's footsteps follow.

"Hey," he says, soft, but you keep walking. "Come on, man, wait."

You don't want to wait. Don't want to stop. If you keep moving maybe you can outrun this feeling. This dread. This shame.

If you stop, you have to face it. Have to answer all the ugly questions bubbling in your sour stomach.

You're never having coffee again.

But he grabs your shoulder, not hard but firm, and you round on him.

"I can't believe you," you tell him.

He throws up his hands. "Hey, it was Reggie who did it."

"But you told him about Farshid."

"It was funny. He got rejected so bad."

A spike of sympathy runs through you. You know what that feels like. How small and useless you felt when Mariana shot you down.

Now that you think about it, that was Brody's fault, wasn't it?

"You're my best friend," you say, but he interrupts you with another "No homo," and you snap.

"Would you quit that? Being friends doesn't make us gay, and there's nothing wrong with it anyway. You're my best friend, but this isn't cool."

"It's just a joke," he says again, crossing his arms, but his face is turning red. "I thought you had a sense of humor."

"And I thought you were a good guy," you snap.

You wish you could take it back. You know Brody's a good guy. He's your best friend.

But what Marshall said keeps running through your head. To try to do better.

And you think about what Farshid said, too. That you've never stood up to Brody, even when he's gone too far.

You are now.

Brody's face turns even redder. "Whatever. If I'm so bad, then go tell on me. Tell on both of us. Pick Farshid and Cooper over me. What have they ever done for you? Oh, that's right, ignore you and make you feel like crap. I can't believe you."

He shoves you away, not hard enough to move you, but you step back anyway as he stalks past, even though his class is the other way.

You're breathing hard, like you just did a warm-up in conditioning. You look back toward the hall where Reggie was doing his work, but you don't go check. You don't know what to do.

Brody's your friend.

But he's wrong.

And Reggie's not even your friend. He's just a jerk.

Farshid's not your friend, either. But you can't stop thinking about how small and scared he sounded. He doesn't deserve this.

No one does.

You hear footsteps—sharp, clicky ones, like a teacher wearing heels, so you get moving again, heading back to German. You return the weird spiky helmet hall pass. Take your seat in the front row. Keep your head down. You can't hear a single thing Frau is saying about dative case, even though you know it's certain to be on the next quiz, and you still want to be gut in Deutsch.

Your head is buzzing. Not from caffeine this time but from your thoughts bouncing around like a swarm of bumblebees, all bonking against the glass panes of everything you thought you knew about Brody.

Yeah, he makes gross jokes sometimes. Yeah, he doesn't always know when to keep his mouth shut.

He makes mistakes sometimes, but who doesn't? You've made your share.

That doesn't make him bad. That doesn't make *you* bad. Does it?

You're trying to do better.

Brody's not, though. He's out there, covering for Reggie, acting like you're the jerk for telling them to stop.

He's your friend. Your best friend.

You don't want him to get in trouble.

But this is wrong. He is wrong. He's not a bad guy. But he's doing a bad thing.

You can't breathe. And you still feel hot all over. And sick to your stomach.

You don't know, you don't know, you don't know—

"Dayton?" Frau asks, and though her voice is soft and round, it cracks like a whip. You sit up straight.

You're still shaking, and you don't know if it's fear or that horrible coffee anymore, but you clear your throat.

"I need to go to the office."

26
FARSHID

YOU'RE HALFWAY THROUGH YOUR QUIZ IN BIO WHEN MX. LEE'S walkie-talkie beeps, and even though they keep the volume low so you can all focus on filling out the little grids of how dominant and recessive traits might be applied to an imaginary person, you're pretty sure you make out your name.

You look up, but then you look right back down, because you don't want to seem like you're cheating, trying to crib off anyone else's quiz. But it feels like a spider's crawling up your neck, the way your skin prickles, wondering if you really *did* hear your name, and whether everyone else did, too, and what's happening.

You keep filling out your quiz, but you're pretty sure you're doing it wrong, so you start erasing when a shadow falls over you.

Mx. Lee's soft belly rests on your desk as they lean over. "Come talk to me when you finish," they say, and your shoulders tense up.

You grip your pencil tighter, clicking it a couple of times even though you don't need more lead, so then you have to click and hold and push the lead back inside. You nod and swallow and try to finish.

When you do—you're worried you only managed a C—you take it up to Mx. Lee's desk.

"I'm done," you manage to say, though your voice sounds weird in your ears, and your throat feels tight.

Mx. Lee takes the quiz and says, "Go pack up your stuff. When the bell rings, we're going to the office."

The office?

You've never been sent to the office, much less *taken* there. What did you do? What do they think you did? Is Cooper mad at you? All you did was ask him out, which, granted, was foolish, but he didn't seem mad, and straight people ask each other out all the time, so why is it that you're the only one getting in trouble?

You think back to this morning, but you didn't do anything in ELA or algebra. Oh God, what if it's not you? What if it's Jina? What if something happened to her? What if she got in trouble, or got hurt, or one of your parents did?

Images of car crashes, fires, tornadoes, every kind of disaster swirl through your mind and settle in your chest until it feels like you're carrying around one of those hundred-pound kettle bells at the gym that you can still barely lift and can only really do a goblet squat with.

The long beep of the bell sounds, and you stare at your hands, waiting for everyone to leave. Mx. Lee comes and stands next to you.

"You all right?" they ask.

You shrug, because your voice is gone.

They say, "Don't worry, you're not in trouble. Come on."

You wish you *were* in trouble, because at least you wouldn't have to worry about everyone else. But you manage to thread your stiff arms through the straps of your backpack and follow your teacher through the halls, eyes focused on their canary-yellow Converses.

You've never been sent to the office before, but you *have* been there, to drop off notes or whatever. It's all obscured windows and quiet talking and shuffling papers and clicking keyboards as you go back, past the main desk and the side hall where the guidance counselors' offices are, until you see the door with the wooden placard that reads *Henry Matthews, PhD, Principal.*

Mx. Lee knocks. Dr. Matthews tells them to come in. So they swing the door open and let you go first.

Dr. Matthews looks up at you and smiles, though his eyes look kind of sad. Maybe it's just his glasses. He nods at Mx. Lee, who backs out, then he gestures for you to take a seat across from his desk . . .

Right next to Dayton, who's staring intently at the pen-filled Meadowbrook mug on the corner of the desk.

Is this about the project? Did you do something wrong? Did he complain about you procrastinating? Ms. Suchecki didn't say anything to you about it.

Did you plagiarize something? You swear you didn't, that everything you put on the slides was in your own words, but what if you accidentally copy-pasted something you didn't mean to? Does that count as copyright infringement? Is that a felony?

"Dayton, can you wait outside?"

Dayton nods and gets up, meeting your eyes for a moment, looking inscrutable, not that you've made much effort to scrute him this year, but you've never seen him looking like this.

When the door clicks shut behind him, Dr. Matthews clears his throat. "Sorry to interrupt your day. I wanted to check in on you."

"Me?" you ask.

He nods. "How are you doing?"

"Fine?"

He nods again. "Anyone bothering you?"

You shake your head. No more than usual. The juniors and seniors act like you don't exist. The sophomores treat you like a little kid, even though they were freshmen just last year. Your classmates . . . well, some are fine, and some are the same jerks you've spent the last six years with. Some are new and quickly figured out you were at the bottom of the social ladder, being Iranian and Bahá'í and *different*.

Dr. Matthews leans back. "All right. Well." He sighs. "A couple of students defaced your locker today. I didn't want you caught off guard. We're going to clean it off, of course, but if you need anything from it, we'll get it. All right?"

You don't understand. Lockers get scratched all the time. Little notes stuck to them. Stickers and decorations.

"Defaced?" you ask, because none of this makes sense.

Dr. Matthews's face is already kind of ruddy, but it turns redder.

"With an offensive word," he says.

One word.

"So I wanted to make sure you knew you were . . . supported here. For who you are."

One word.

Oh God, is he trying to tell you he knows?

This is a nightmare.

"Dayton reported it," he says, sounding . . . impressed? "Which showed great integrity."

You blink at him.

Dayton stood up for you? It doesn't make any sense.

"I'll have to tell your parents, but I wanted to check, ah . . . how much you were comfortable with me discussing with them."

Oh.

He's not sure if your parents know.

Is he worried about you? Does he think they'd disown you or something?

"They know," you say quietly.

"And you're doing okay?" he asks again.

"I'm okay."

You're not okay.

You're a nervous wreck is what you are.

That one word. Scrawled across your locker. You didn't see it but you can picture it, the sharp angles and broad curves against the red metal.

You want to run, you want to scream, you want to hide, you want to hit something.

You don't know what you want.

Except that you want out of this stifling office, with this grown-up who's trying to act like he understands you, with the lingering notes of Dayton's cologne, like he's still right there next to you, with yourself, because you thought you were so brave yesterday but you're not. You're still afraid.

You hate being afraid.

But you say it again: "I'm okay."

ONE, ONE, THREE, YOU SAY TO YOURSELF. JAB, JAB, LEFT HOOK.

One, four, five, four. Jab, right hook, left uppercut, right hook.

You pound the bag, sweat dripping down your temple, stinging your eye where it hits the crease, but you ignore it. Your arms have gone leaden, your fists are throbbing in their wraps and gloves, but you don't stop.

You can't stop.

Bob. Weave. Combo. Combo. Combo.

You picture Reggie's face. Brody's.

Everyone's talking about what they did. What they did to you.

You don't want to hit them, not really. You don't want to hit anyone.

But you're tired of thinking about them. You just want them to go away.

Two, one, two. Cross, jab, cross. The bag bucks on its chain, swings away and back, but your timing is off, and your next jab barely connects, sending the bag into a spin. You grab it to stop it, leaning your sweating forehead against it, but it's heavier than you remember. And are your legs shaking?

You breathe hard, trying to catch your breath, trying to push off and get back into your stance, but once your arms slip away from the bag you can't bring yourself to lift them again. You feel weak.

You think you're going to throw up.

Instead you swallow it down and manage to bring your fists up again.

"Whoa, whoa," Coach Nico says.

You drop your hands and glance back toward the entrance. He's still in his outside clothes, jeans and a polo shirt with some company logo on the left breast, from his day job when he's not coaching boxing. "You look like you need a break."

You shake your head.

"I'm fine."

You've still got another thirty minutes, plus weights after. Today's leg day, and you never miss leg day. Not ever.

But Coach Nico drops his duffel bag on the front desk and comes over to you, grabbing the bag and holding it steady and looking right at you.

You meet his gaze, his blue eyes shadowed by his low-drawn brow, but you don't know what he sees when he looks at you. You're not sure you want to know. You like your coach, but he doesn't know everything about you, and you don't know if you're ready for him to yet.

"It wasn't a suggestion," he finally says. "Come on."

Something in his voice tells you he means business, so you drop your arms, try to scoop up your empty water bottle from where it's leaning against one of the posts, but you can't quite grab it with your gloves on, so he leans down and picks it up for you, giving it a shake.

"You need more water," he says, walking you to the fountain, where he fills it up for you, and then he leads you past the others working out, a woman in her forties on the speed bag, one in her twenties on the pec deck, a guy in his twenties doing box jumps. He settles on the cubby bench and pats it for you to sit next to him, then hands you your water bottle.

You drink and drink and drink.

"You doing okay?" he asks.

"I'm fine," you say, too quick, too aggressive.

His eyebrows rise, which really shows off the little bald scar on his right one.

"I'm okay," you say again, firmer. You are.

"I'm worried about you," he says, and you pause halfway through undoing your glove.

He takes your arm and opens up the Velcro, pulls off the glove, then gestures for your other arm. You let him, but you have a hard time keeping your arm higher than your chest.

"Here. Stay put." He sets your gloves on the bench, gets up, comes back a moment later with his duffel bag, which is weird because you could swear all you did was blink, but he definitely went somewhere and came back. He pulls out a chocolate bar. Not a protein one, but a candy one. A Snickers. "Eat this."

You shake your head. Candy is a definite no. Too much sugar, and the macros are all wrong, and—

"Farshid. You're not eating right."

"I'm good," you say. You are. You track every meal, all your macros, you—

"When's the last time you had a slice of pizza?" he asks. "Or a cookie?"

You gave them up. You're not bulking right now, you're trying to build lean muscle.

Coach Nico blows out a long breath and looks away from you. He runs a hand over his buzzed hair and blows out a raspberry. "I don't know how to do this."

"Huh?"

He looks back at you, and there's something new in his gaze, something that gets your hackles on the rise.

"You know why I don't compete anymore?" he asks.

You shake your head.

"All the weigh-ins," he says. "I'd track all my eating. Starve myself. Dehydrate myself to make weight. Maybe I'd win in the ring, maybe I'd lose, but you know what I got a hundred percent of the time?"

You shake your head again.

"An unhappy wife and kids. And a miserable me." He sighs. "I'm so proud of all the progress you've made, but I'm worried about you, too. You're fourteen. You're not supposed to be jacked. You're not supposed to be counting calories. You're supposed to be eating junk food with your friends. You're supposed to be growing up."

You can't eat junk food. That'll ruin everything. That'll . . .

He rubs his head again, stares at the woman on the speed bag, who's just doubled her tempo and is going to town. She's lean and strong and truly S-tier, her abs showing beneath her sports bra. You wonder what her food plan is like. You're trying to mentally calculate her body fat percentage when Coach Nico clears his throat.

"You know what body dysmorphia is?"

You turn back to him. Shake your head.

"It's when you have a messed-up sense of what your own body looks like."

"What?" You can see yourself in the mirror. "I know what I look like."

"I'm not explaining this well." He rubs his chin. It's the tiniest bit crooked from his days in the ring. "Listen. I'm not your doctor, and I'm not your therapist. But I *am* your coach, and I *do* care about your well-being. Not just about how hard you can hit but about how happy you are. And I really think you need to talk to someone about this, because I don't think it's healthy for you, Farshid."

"I'm fine."

You are fine.

You are.

You're not scared anymore. You came out to your mom, to some of your friends. Soon the whole school will know.

"I'm gay," you blurt out.

You wish you hadn't.

But Coach Nico laughs and musses your hair, then makes a face and shakes the sweat off his hand. He pulls a towel out of his bag, wipes his hands off, then pats your back.

"That's cool," he says. "Thank you for telling me. But that doesn't change anything. I want you to let me talk to your parents about this."

"Don't—"

"And until you do," he adds, an edge to his voice. "I'm not coaching you anymore. I'm supposed to be helping you, not making you unhealthy."

"You can't do that!"

He shakes his head. "I should've done it sooner. But better late than never."

You stare at him. How can he do this to you?

His eyes soften, though.

"Even the Energizer Bunny needs fuel," he says. "I'm not trying to punish you. I'm trying to help you. I can even give your parents the name of my therapist."

You shake your head. "*You* see a therapist?"

He shrugs. "I've got problems. Who doesn't? It never hurts to get help."

You sigh. He pushes the Snickers your way.

You shouldn't.

You really shouldn't.

But it does look good.

"I'll split it with you," you say softly.

He nods and breaks off part for you.

Maybe he's right.

Maybe you do need a little help.

27

DAYTON

YOU MISS BRODY.

You miss him at your locker before school.

You miss him at lunch.

You miss him during passing periods, when you'd walk by each other as you hustled to opposite ends of the building and barely have time to bump fists.

You especially miss him in conditioning, because now you have to jog alone during warm-ups.

You did your best not to make a big deal out of it that day. Frau pressed you on why you needed to go to the office, so you told her you saw a defaced locker on the way back from the bathroom. You didn't tell her you knew who did it. But she handed back the little helmet pass and sent you on your way.

You had to talk to one of the admins before you could actually get anywhere, but finally Dr. Matthews asked you to step into his office.

You told him the whole thing.

You made sure to emphasize it was Reggie you actually saw with the Sharpie, Reggie doing the actual defacing, but it didn't seem to matter.

Brody and Reggie both got suspended. Out of school, this time. Seven days.

The district minimum, because of the whole zero-tolerance thing.

You don't know if Brody knows you told on him. After two days, he still hasn't answered any of your texts. You don't know if it's because he's mad at you or because he's grounded.

You can't decide what you're supposed to feel.

You betrayed your best friend.

A friend's supposed to stick with you, right? Not dump you, like Tyler and Cooper did. A friend's supposed to call you in, not call you out, right?

But you tried that. He didn't listen. And you couldn't let him hurt someone, not even Farshid.

Farshid, who missed fourth hour today but is back now for seventh. You want to ask him where he was. If he's okay. But the two of you don't talk about that. You don't talk about anything except your project, and that's fine, really.

You don't need him to be your friend. You don't need him to like you. You don't even need him to not hate you. It's not about him.

It's about what's right.

After conditioning, when you're changed and you've reapplied your fragrance, you bump into Cooper at the door.

You're about to move past, but he raises a hand.

"Hey," he says.

"Hey." Cooper's got his spring fragrance on, too. He always picked good ones. "Light Blue?"

"Good nose."

You shrug and keep moving, but he follows you toward the student exit. Marshall doesn't have practice this afternoon, so you can get a ride home from him.

You and Cooper spent all of middle school waiting together after school: for the regular bus, for the activities bus, for your parents or his or both. You thought you'd spend all of high school doing the same. At least until you could drive.

But that's not how this year has turned out.

He's still beside you when you stop next to the bike racks, where there's this little brick wall that's exactly the right height for you to rest your backpack on it without actually taking it off.

Cooper's quiet as you both watch the tide of juniors and seniors headed to their cars.

You don't know what's going on. This isn't middle school. You're not friends anymore.

"You need something?" you ask, in what you hope is a neutral tone.

"Farshid told me what you did," he says.

"What?"

"About Brody and Reggie."

"Oh." You squeeze the straps of your backpack. You don't know what to say to that.

You know you did the right thing, but you still feel like crap anyway.

Cooper doesn't seem to know what else to say, either.

Finally he says, "I'm glad you did it."

You shrug. You didn't do it for him.

And then he says: "I miss being friends."

You look at him then, really look. His eyes are big and dark and shiny, like obsidian. He hasn't really looked at you in a long time.

"You're the one who dropped me," you point out.

Cooper does his fish face, blowing up his cheeks real big and letting out a sigh. You used to make fun of him for it. Nothing too mean. It was just funny is all.

"Yeah," he says. "I'm sorry."

Sorry doesn't erase what happened. Sorry doesn't make anything better.

"Thanks, I guess."

You don't know what else to say. You don't know if you forgive him. You don't know how you feel about him or Tyler.

Except you do. You're angry.

"You didn't even give me a chance," you say. "Neither of you did. You didn't let me try to fix it or make it up to anyone. We were best friends for years, and you acted like it meant nothing. Like I was toxic because of one mistake. And yeah, it was a bad one. Yeah, I messed up. But I didn't deserve to be cut out like that. With no way back. That wasn't cool. That wasn't fair."

Cooper's eyes get bigger and wider as you go. You feel like a helium balloon that sprang a leak, your voice getting higher and higher, your breath getting thinner and thinner, until finally you run out of words and fall silent.

You think he's going to turn around and ditch you again.

Instead he looks down at his Jordans. His school ones, because he wouldn't risk scuffing his nice ones.

"You're right," he mutters. "You're right. We messed up, too. You didn't deserve that."

You wait for it to feel better. For his admission to unlock something inside to make the past six months make sense. But it doesn't.

It still hurts.

"I'm sorry, Dayton," he says, looking back up. "I want to try to make it up. Tyler does, too. You think we can try again?"

He holds out his fist for you to bump.

A peace offering.

A chance to fix things.

You stare at it, but you don't move.

You're not sure if you're ready to bump it back or not.

YOU STILL HAVEN'T HEARD FROM BRODY, SO YOU ASK YOUR DAD IF he can give you a ride over to check on him.

"I can't just drop everything to be your driver," he says. "Ask your brother."

You don't want to. Marshall doesn't like Brody. But to your surprise, he agrees without complaint.

"You want me to wait for you?" he asks when you pull up outside Brody's house.

You don't know. You don't know if Brody will let you in. Or even talk to you. You stare out the window at his house. It's a normal color for a house, unlike the bright peachy orange of your own. Apparently it was like that when your family moved in—you were a baby back then—and your mom liked how it gave the house character, so it's still that weird color now.

Brody's house is gray-green, and all the neighbors more or less match: gray-blue, gray-red, gray-gray, even a gray-purple on the corner.

Maybe your mom had a little bit of a point.

You grab the door handle. "Maybe wait at the end of the block? I'll let you know?"

Marshall bites his lip and nods. Before you get out, he stops you.

"Hey."

"Yeah?"

"I'm proud of you, you know."

You roll your eyes, but Marshall keeps looking at you.

"I'm serious."

Warmth settles in your stomach. "Thanks."

Brody's parents are really into landscaping: The front yard has a winding path that curves between budding shrubs and flower beds. The first time you came over, the shrubs were full and green and carved into sharp lines, and the flowers had already bloomed and died, and the trees were starting to turn. Now the shrubs are budding, the flower beds have fresh shoots poking out, and the trees are starting to blossom.

You don't want this to be the last time you come here.

You step up to the door and ring the bell and wait. Did Brody even get your message that you were swinging by? If he *is* grounded, you hope his parents will let you talk to him anyway. Even if you have to do an awkward through-the-storm-door type thing.

You glance back at the street, but your brother has indeed gone down to the end of the block, one driveway away from the stop sign.

Brody finally opens the door. He's in plaid pajama pants, which you've never seen him in before. But maybe he doesn't have to show off his gains to anyone when he's at home.

"Hey," you say.

You can't tell if he's happy to see you or not. His hand is still on the door. And he hasn't opened the storm door. So you reach for it and swing it open, though you have to take an awkward step back, off the front step, and then forward again.

"What are you doing here?"

"I wanted to talk. Are you allowed?"

He shrugs, but he doesn't let you in. Instead he steps outside, so you take another step back, and you have to let go of the storm door. He manages to step out of the way and let it close behind him.

"So talk," he says, arms crossed over his *Star Wars* shirt.

"You doing okay?" you ask.

He rolls his eyes. "Did you actually need something?"

"No! I mean, I really did want to see if you're okay." You scratch at your head. You know what you want to say, but you don't know how.

"What do you think? I've got a seven-day suspension. My parents are furious. My grades are gonna take a hit, too. And the guy who did it to me showed up at my house like we're still friends."

You flinch.

"I'm still your friend," you say.

"Friends don't rat each other out."

"I did what I thought was right." No. "What I know was right. You're my friend, Brody, but what you and Reggie were doing was wrong."

"We weren't hurting anyone," he says. "Why, are you a homo?"

You sigh. "Brody . . ."

"Just get out of here. I'm done with you."

"I'm sorry you got in trouble," you say. And you are. But Brody wasn't listening. You didn't have any other choice. Not one you could live with, at least.

If you hadn't told on him, things would've been worse. For Farshid. For everyone else like Farshid, too.

"I really am. But friends are supposed to make each other better. Keep each other from making mistakes. I hope you can forgive me someday. You're my best friend. I don't want that to end just because of this."

His face softens, like he's unclenched his jaw. Even his arms go a little slack, before he crosses them even tighter.

"Well, I don't forgive you," he says. "You screwed me over. Now leave me alone."

You expected this, you think.

Or at least you had a feeling it would go this way.

Brody's your friend. Well, he was. And he's been a good friend.

But maybe he's not a very good guy right now.

You hope someday he'll forgive you. That you can be friends again.

And you hope he'll be better. Not just for your sake, or Farshid's sake, or anyone else's sake, but for Brody's own. You don't know how to explain any of that to him, though, not when he's not willing to listen. Not when he's going back inside and closing the door in your face. On your friendship.

You almost want to cry. This isn't how things were supposed to go.

This isn't how your first year of high school was meant to turn out.

But it is what it is.

If you could go back to Tuesday, when you found him and

Reggie, you'd try harder. You'd beg or plead or do anything to get him to stop. But if he didn't, if you faced the same choice . . . you'd do it all again.

You want to be the kind of guy who does the right thing.

And for the first time in a long while, you're pretty sure you are.

28

FARSHID

"YOU'LL NEVER BELIEVE WHO GOT BACK TOGETHER," NOUR WHISPERS in your ear as you look over the cookie tray. You waffle for a good thirty seconds before settling on a snickerdoodle, truly an S-tier cookie.

You still pick the smallest one you can find, but, well. You only had your first therapy appointment yesterday. You're not supposed to change overnight, just make small steps toward getting . . .

Better feels like a loaded word, but maybe it's right. Maybe you are getting better.

Your parents were surprisingly supportive about the whole therapy thing. Maybe they've become more Americanized than you realized, or maybe Coach Nico did a better job explaining things to them than you did, or maybe your mom was biting her tongue the whole time to hold in an *I told you so!*

You didn't get how worried she was about you.

You haven't told anyone at school about it, though, not even Nour or Cooper. Not because it's a secret, not because you're ashamed, but because you're simply not ready to share yet. It feels like you've had to share so much of yourself lately, sometimes with complete strangers, even if they are well-meaning professionals, so you want to hold on to this for yourself, for a little while at least.

"Who?" you ask around a mouthful of cinnamon and sugar.

"June and Marie!"

"Oh." June and Marie have broken up and gotten back together almost as many times as they've both dyed their hair this year. Right now June's is bubblegum pink and Marie's is purple, but her brown roots are showing. "Good for them."

Nour rolls her eyes. Ever since you came out to her (if her finding out about what was scrawled on your locker and you shrugging counts as coming out), she's been even more disappointed in you not caring about gossip.

"What's the point of a gay best friend if you don't give me any tea?"

You raise your eyebrows.

"Metaphorically," she says, raising her cup of literal tea that you provided her.

"Can't I just be your regular best friend?"

She gives you a shove, but you don't move. You're still working out, though Coach Nico made you promise to stick to only one workout a day, plus two rest days a week, and he said he told the front desk at the gym to not let you in if you showed up too often. You don't know if he actually did, but you're not going to test him.

You don't want to test him.

And also, not waking up at five in the morning every day has actually been really nice.

You and Nour hover in the corner, Nour filling you in on the rest of the gossip she's been holding on to. She refused to share any of it over text during spring break, so now there's a backlog. You nod along and keep an eye on the door as the rest of RC slowly files in, grabbing cookies and napkins and greeting friends they haven't seen yet today.

You give Hope a little nod and smile when she enters. You thought she might be mad at you, given the whole rejection thing, but when you told her the real reason you didn't want to go out with her, she thanked you for being honest and told you she'd support you.

Nour is halfway through a story about a senior prank gone wrong when you spot Cooper at the door, hovering in the hall, talking to someone. Things have been weird between you two ever since you asked him out and he turned you down. Not bad, but weird, and you know it's your fault, because you like him as a friend, and you also *like* like him, and you don't know how to not like him like that, but that's not his problem to deal with, it's yours. You don't want to lose him as a friend, but you don't know how to not hurt every time he smiles at you.

Still, when he catches your eye and grins, it doesn't hurt as bad this time. Maybe someday the two of you can be back to how it was.

He looks toward the hall, says something, reaches out, and drags someone in with him.

Not just someone.

Dayton.

Nour's jaw drops, sending cookie crumbles tumbling onto her keffiyeh before she brushes them off. "What's he doing here?"

"I don't know."

You and Dayton didn't magically become friends after the whole locker thing. You did your presentation together, and that was that. You still don't talk much, and you're fine with that. Yeah, he did the right thing, but that doesn't erase the wrong he's done, does it?

Maybe it does, because some people smile at him, welcome him to RC, clap him on the back like he's some sort of hero for turning in his ex–best friend. But then again, some folks are hanging back, looking at him warily, because he's still the guy who shouted a slur at an assembly, too.

He spots you, and his cheeks flush, but he doesn't look away, and you don't, either, not until Cooper takes him to the cookie table and you can breathe again.

"Well. Maybe he's trying to do better," Nour says.

"Maybe."

You don't know how to feel about that. You don't want to deal with him, here, the one place in school you can truly relax, where you don't have to have any hackles at all.

But he's coming your way.

"Hey," Cooper says, smiling at you again, and he still smells nice, like always. Dayton does, too. You've noticed that in history lately. Maybe he's always smelled nice, and you've been unwilling to admit it. He and Cooper are friends again, and you don't know how to feel about that, either, because him and Cooper being friends, and you and Cooper being friends, feels like it shouldn't mix.

"Hey," you say.

Dayton swallows his bite of chocolate chip cookie.

"Hey," he says.

You should say *hey* back, but your voice isn't working. Your throat has clamped shut.

Dayton hurt you. He was friends with people who hurt you. He and Reggie and Brody made this year a nightmare. Made you afraid to walk down the halls, made you afraid of yourself. But he also stood up to them, eventually. He tried to keep your secret.

And he's here now. Doing what you told him.

Taking action.

So, what? Are you supposed to be cool with it, cool with him, like nothing ever happened? And if you're not cool with it, does that make you the problem?

He's still looking at you, and he looks hopeful and wary and sad, those big blue eyes of his wide and open.

You've spent all year feeling afraid, feeling paranoid, feeling helpless, but you're not anymore.

Now he's the one who's afraid, who's nervous, who's not sure if he's welcome or wanted.

One word from you can shape his future. You're the one with the power.

How are you going to use it?

Acknowledgments

This book would not exist without my agent, Molly O'Neill, who, when I described the experience that inspired this book, asked me if there was a story there. Turns out you were right! Thank you to the entire Root Literary team for supporting my career: Holly Root, Taylor Haggerty, Kurestin Armada, Jasmine Brown, Samantha Fabien, Melanie Figueroa, Gabrielle Greenstein, Stacy Jenson, Alyssa Maltese, Kat Miller, and Jessica Saint Jean. Thank you to Heather Baror-Shapiro for sharing *One Word, Six Letters* with the world, and to Debbie Deuble Hill for everything you do!

Thank you to my editor, Dana Chidiac, for grasping the heart of this book so quickly and for helping me bring it to its best form. Thank you to Valery Badio, assistant editor extraordinaire, for your insights and help and all the behind-the-scenes work.

Thank you to Samira Iravani for the exquisite cover design and art direction. My jaw hit the floor the first time I saw this cover.

Thanks to the entire team at Henry Holt Books for Young Readers, who embraced this book wholeheartedly: Ann Marie Wong, editorial director; Jean Feiwel, publisher; Alexei Esikoff and Lelia Mander, managing editorial; Melissa Zar, Johanna Allen, Robby Chandler-Brown, and their teams, marketing; Mary Van Akin and her team, school and library marketing; Molly Ellis, Chantal Gersch, and the publicity team; Shawn Foster and her team, sales.

Thank you to Esther de Araujo for producing the audiobook

version of *One Word, Six Letters*, and to Major Curda and Arya Shahi for bringing it to life.

I could not have written this book without the space and time afforded to me by the MacDowell Fellowship. Thank you to all my fellows, the entire MacDowell team, Lio Min for recommending MacDowell to me in the first place, and Veltin Studio for being the perfect place to work.

Thank you to all the usual suspects (at this point you know who you are, and there are too many of you to list here). Thank you to every bookseller, librarian, educator, influencer, and reader who has picked up one of my books or put it into the hands of another.

And last of all, as always—thank you to you, dear reader. I do this for you.

About the Author

Adib Khorram is a queer Iranian-American author. His critically acclaimed novels include *Darius the Great Is Not Okay*, *Darius the Great Deserves Better*, *Kiss & Tell*, and *The Breakup Lists*. When he's not writing, he enjoys yoga, figure skating, electric guitar, food, wine, tea, board games, and explaining to people why Kansas City has the best barbecue. You can find him on online at adibkhorram.com.